YORK NOTES

The Go-Between

L.P. Hartley

Notes by Mary Pascoe

 Longman   York Press

YORK PRESS
322 Old Brompton Road, London SW5 9JH

ADDISON WESLEY LONGMAN LIMITED
Edinburgh Gate, Harlow,
Essex CM20 2JE, United Kingdom
Associated companies, branches and representatives throughout the world

First published 1998

ISBN 0–582–36842–1

Designed by Vicki Pacey, Trojan Horse, London
Illustrated by Susan Scott
Phototypeset by Gem Graphics, Trenance, Mawgan Porth, Cornwall
Colour reproduction and film output by Spectrum Colour
Produced by Addison Wesley Longman China Limited, Hong Kong

Contents

PREFACE

York Notes are designed to give you a broader perspective on works of literature studied at GCSE and equivalent levels. We have carried out extensive research into the needs of the modern literature student prior to publishing this new edition. Our research showed that no existing series fully met students' requirements. Rather than present a single authoritative approach, we have provided alternative viewpoints, empowering students to reach their own interpretations of the text. York Notes provide a close examination of the work and include biographical and historical background, summaries, glossaries, analyses of characters, themes, structure and language, cultural connections and literary terms.

If you look at the Contents page you will see the structure for the series. However, there's no need to read from the beginning to the end as you would with a novel, play, poem or short story. Use the Notes in the way that suits you. Our aim is to help you with your understanding of the work, not to dictate how you should learn.

York Notes are written by English teachers and examiners, with an expert knowledge of the subject. They show you how to succeed in coursework and examination assignments, guiding you through the text and offering practical advice. Questions and comments will extend, test and reinforce your knowledge. Attractive colour design and illustrations improve clarity and understanding, making these Notes easy to use and handy for quick reference.

York Notes are ideal for:
- Essay writing
- Exam preparation
- Class discussion

The author of these Notes, Mary Pascoe, is an experienced teacher, moderator and senior examiner. She has co-authored a number of text books and until recently was Head of English at Winstanley College, Wigan. She has just completed post-graduate language research at Liverpool University.

The text used in these Notes is the Penguin Twentieth-Century Classics edition, edited by Douglas Brooks-Davies, 1997.

Health Warning: **This study guide will enhance your understanding, but should not replace the reading of the original text and/or study in class.**

PART ONE

INTRODUCTION

HOW TO STUDY A NOVEL

You have bought this book because you wanted to study a novel on your own. This may supplement classwork.

- You will need to read the novel several times. Start by reading it quickly for pleasure, then read it slowly and carefully. Further readings will generate new ideas and help you to memorise the details of the story.
- Make careful notes on themes, plot and characters of the novel. The plot will change some of the characters. Who changes?
- The novel may not present events chronologically. Does the novel you are reading begin at the beginning of the story or does it contain flashbacks and a muddled time sequence? Can you think why?
- How is the story told? Is it narrated by one of the characters or by an all-seeing ('omniscient') narrator?
- Does the same person tell the story all the way through? Or do we see the events through the minds and feelings of a number of different people.
- Which characters does the narrator like? Which characters do you like or dislike? Do your sympathies change during the course of the book? Why? When?
- Any piece of writing (including your notes and essays) is the result of thousands of choices. No book had to be written in just one way: the author could have chosen other words, other phrases, other characters, other events. How could the author of your novel have written the story differently? If events were recounted by a minor character how would this change the novel?

Studying on your own requires self-discipline and a carefully thought-out work plan in order to be effective. Good luck.

L.P. Hartley's background

Note the ways in which Leo's life reflects L.P. Hartley's own.

Although *The Go-Between* is not an autobiography, there are a number of ways in which the story echoes his own life. He was born in 1895, into a well-to-do middle-class family (his father was a solicitor) but his maternal grandparents had a farm in Lincolnshire. He vividly remembered the summer of 1900 because the family moved house in that year. He was educated at home until he went to boarding school at thirteen, (his school was called Northdown) but, unlike Leo, he had two sisters. He went on a visit to stay with a school friend, with whom he shared a room, and wrote home explaining he did not want to accept their invitation to stay longer. He remembered a cricket match, and his letters home from school show he took a keen interest in the results of the school soccer matches. He also had a good singing voice as a child. At one time he even lived in a house called 'Court House', near Salisbury, and learned to swim only in his teens. There is even speculation that he partly based the character of Mrs Maudsley on his strong-willed mother. After Northdown he went to public school (Harrow) and then won a scholarship to Oxford University, though his education was interrupted by the First World War. Hartley joined the army, but did not see active service. After completing his education, he made his living as a writer and as a reviewer. He never married.

As well as lots of short stories, he wrote a total of seventeen novels, two of which (including *The Go-Between*) won prizes. *The Go-Between* (1953) and another novel, *The Hireling* (1957) were made into successful films. Among his other novels, a trilogy called *The Shrimp and the Anemone* (1944); *The Sixth Heaven* (1946); and *Eustace and Hilda* (1947) are also stories about childhood and growing up. The past and memories of the past fascinated him, and he was a great admirer of Emily Brontë's novel *Wuthering Heights* (1847) which also tells the past through memories and flashbacks.

The poet John Betjeman described *The Go-Between* as L.P. Hartley's best novel. His achievements were honoured by his being awarded the CBE in 1956. He died in 1972.

CONTEXT & SETTING

The Boer War was being fought far away in South Africa at the time. Think about the way it is included in the novel.

The main part of the novel takes place in late-Victorian England. Victoria's long reign of over sixty years saw many changes and improvements in education, medicine, health and housing, as well as many developments in science, engineering and technology. The British Empire covered a very large area of the world and Britain was a major world power of the status of the USA today. Exports and trade brought great wealth to the country. There were no signs that prosperity and influence could ever decline. The year 1900 not only marked the beginning of a new decade, but also a new century, and Leo's high hopes for the century were shared by many people who felt that things could only continue to get better. You might like to think of how people are looking forward now to not only the next century but also to the next millennium.

The house seems like a far-off world to a modern reader.

Brandham Hall is typical of the large country house of the period. The Hall sees itself as separate from the neighbouring village; another world, in fact, with its gardens, parkland and farms. It is run by a large number of servants, who live in a separate part of the house and who are deferential even to a young boy like Leo. He is not, for example, expected to pick up or fold his clothes. The house is full of an ever-changing company of visitors, and only Mr Maudsley does not seem to idle his time away in a variety of leisure pursuits such as croquet, picnicking, bathing and visiting other similar families. Upper-class women like Marion led particularly restricted, if sheltered, lives. They did not have the vote, nor were they, other than in exceptional circumstances, able to earn their own living. Their clothes with their long heavy skirts and tight waists were also restricting. Even when swimming, they wore voluminous bathing dresses. Marion's riding of Leo's birthday bicycle would have been considered a daring, even slightly shocking action, since she would need to show her legs in some way. Emotions were expected to be repressed as well as bodies covered up, and Leo, although unusually close to his mother for the period, finds it impossible to confide in her.

Note the ways in which the real events of the twentieth century reflect the mood of disappointment for both Leo and Marion.

But at the end of the novel we see that all Leo's hopes for a golden future have been dashed. The coming of the First World War in 1914 swept away this privileged world. So many young men were killed (Marion, for example, loses both her brothers) and the economic troubles of the 1920s and 1930s ruined many fortunes. People were no longer prepared to work for low wages as domestic servants. The rise of trade unions and equal rights for women also changed the relationship between social classes and between the sexes. The Second World War brought even more social change, as well as the horrors of Nazi concentration camps and the atom bomb. After the war, high rates of taxation made looking after houses like Brandham Hall a great burden; Marion's grandson has let off most of the house to a girls' school.

But in 1900 social changes were already on the way. On the one hand there are the Maudsleys who are not actually the owners of Brandham Hall (although Mr Maudsley has made enough money to lease it). He is typical of the rising upper-middle class, who have had to work for their money, rather than inherit it, but who now want to live the kind of lifestyle once reserved for the aristocracy. His children, particularly Marion, are expected to make marriages which will further enhance their social status. On the other hand, Trimingham is an aristocrat, but the fact that he has let his home suggests that his income from inherited wealth is no longer sufficient to maintain it. Putting aside whatever his feelings are towards Marion, he will gain financially from the marriage. His career as an army officer is typical of the kind of public service expected of his class. (Army officers at this time were not well paid and needed a private income.) He has an easy grace and feels secure of his position in society, in contrast for example to Marcus who is very aware of all the details of what was regarded as correct behaviour. His concern about making mistakes is typical of those who have moved up the social ladder. Leo, too, on a lower rung of the ladder, learns that for him, it is important to obey all the rules, so as not to look like a 'cad'. Children at this time were expected to behave as nearly as possible like adults; the 'teenager' had not yet been invented!

Think about how ideas of class and social status run through the story.

Society at this time was full of rules which governed every aspect of behaviour including a strict dress code. Life in the upper-middle classes and above was very formal. Leo for example, only once in his visit ever hears Mr Maudsley call his wife by her first name, and Leo is very anxious to give Trimingham his proper title. There were clear cut social divisions. Ted, for example, calls himself a 'working farmer' to distinguish himself from a 'gentleman farmer' like Trimingham but he is still higher in status than the farm-workers or other villagers, and Denys recognises he had to be civil to him. Marcus on the other hand makes very rude remarks about the villagers after the cricket concert.

Leo himself, as the son of a bank manager, and his widowed mother are both very aware of their less secure place in society and Mrs Colston realises it will not be possible to invite Marcus back to their house. Even Ted is deferential to Leo once he realises he is a guest at the Hall. Putting aside any moral implications, Marion's affair with Ted was a very shocking breach of these clear-cut social divisions. At the concert it is observed that they make a fine couple, but, due to the difference in their status, marriage between them is out if the question, as they both know. Romantic love is all very well, but marriage is also a question of money and status.

PART TWO

SUMMARIES

GENERAL SUMMARY

Part one: key experiences and background

Leo Colston is in his sixties. He is going through some old papers when he discovers a diary for 1900, the year he was thirteen. In unlocking the diary, he unlocks memories of a summer that was to affect the rest of his life.

Initially he remembers his first months at boarding school. A lonely child, he is teased and bullied. Having no-one to turn to, in desperation he writes a 'curse' on his tormentors in his diary, and they are seriously injured. His status in the school rises, and he becomes a popular figure, especially when he claims that his 'magic' caused the measles outbreak which ends the summer term early. He is invited to stay with a school friend, Marcus Maudsley. When he arrives at Brandham Hall, he finds it difficult to fit into a much grander way of life, especially as he and Marcus are the only children in a large house full of adult visitors. He much prefers exploring the back of the house, and the neglected buildings there than joining in the social round.

His discomfort increases as the weather turns very hot and he has no summer clothes. He is rescued by Marcus's sister who, guessing his predicament, takes him to buy a complete set of new clothes which transforms Leo's whole outlook on life. He becomes a devoted admirer of Marion, delighting in her attention. Another guest arrives; Trimingham, a badly scarred war hero who, he later realises, is a viscount, and actually owns the house which the Maudsley's have leased.

Part two: *Leo becomes* *entangled in* *the* *relationships* *of the three* *central* *characters*	Exploring on his own as Marcus is confined to bed, suspected of having measles, Leo wanders into a farmyard where he gashes his leg sliding on the haystack. The angry farmer, Ted Burgess, becomes friendly and helpful once he finds where Leo is staying. Leo takes a 'business' letter from him to Marion, and both of then swear him to secrecy. Leo then enjoys regularly taking messages between Marion and Ted, and also between Trimingham and Marion. He is flattered by all the attention but does not understand the world of adult behaviour and emotions he is involved in until he reads part of a love letter between Ted and Marion, and Ted tries to explain something of their emotions.
Part three: *from triumph* *to disaster;* *Leo's vanity* *takes a tumble*	During the annual cricket match between the Hall and the village, Leo begins to understand that more is at stake than just a game. Leo helps his side to win by catching out Ted, after Ted has nearly gained victory for the village. Leo feels a bit guilty but Ted generously praises him. A supper and concert follow in the village hall, where at one point, Ted and Marion take the platform together. Leo also gives a star performance (with Marion's help) and ends the day feeling completely elated.

As Marion's engagement to Trimingham is about to be announced he wrongly assumes he will not be taking any more messages to Ted, especially as Marcus has now recovered, but Marion flies into a rage when he tries to explain this. He is further worried by the story Trimingham tells him about the death of an ancestor in a duel over a woman.

When he takes the letter, he antagonises Ted by nagging him to explain about sex and Ted orders him off the farm. Doubly hurt, he writes home, asking to be recalled early. Marcus also offends him by saying everyone (including Marion) thinks he is naïve so they are going to give him a green bicycle as a present.

Part four:
Leo cannot
avert the final
catastrophe of
which he is
also a victim

The strain seems to be affecting everyone. Leo thinks that his leaving will put everything right, but his mother's letter suggests he should complete his stay. It seems only a matter of time before the love affair is discovered. To stave off what he fears will be some kind of fatality, he falsifies an oral message from Ted. Marion erupts in a fury when she thinks Trimingham is trying to get Ted to volunteer for the army (though he does not, in fact, know about the letters). She confides all her unhappiness to an increasingly desperate Leo. He does not know whom to blame, but decides he must end the affair in the only way he has left; by casting a spell as he did at school.

The weather is cooler the next day (his birthday), and he takes this as a good sign but things quickly go wrong as Mrs Maudsley clearly suspects Leo's role as a go-between. She nearly gets him to confess but a thunderstorm interrupts their conversation. Marion is mysteriously late for the birthday tea, and Mrs Maudsley suddenly forces Leo to go with her to the outhouses where they find Marion and Ted making love. Ted goes home and shoots himself and both Mrs Maudsley and Leo have nervous breakdowns.

Part five:
the ghosts of
the past are
laid to rest

Leo recovers but leads a very dull, 'safe' life not wanting to risk any further emotional involvement. The novel finishes with the adult Leo returning to Norfolk to find out what has happened to everyone, and to try to re-assess his own part in the events. He meets Marion's grandson, and agrees to act as a go-between for Marion for one last time – hopefully to good effect.

Part one

Prologue

'The past is another country: they do things differently there'

When the novel opens the narrator and central character of the story, Leo Colston, is in his sixties and the date is 1952. He has found a box containing some childhood possessions, including a diary for the year 1900 which arouses in him memories which he has buried for the past fifty years.

Leo is particularly attracted to the drawing of the virgin (virgo).

He remembers how he was fascinated the signs of the zodiac (see illustration on p. 81) in the diary, and his special hopes for the twentieth century He was about to become a teenager and no longer wanted to identify himself with his own sign, Leo, because it was an animal. He was searching for a more grown-up figure to model himself on; the archer (Sagittarius) or the water-carrier (Aquarius). He is reluctant to open the diary because he feels that the events it records are responsible for his rather lonely and unhappy life and his disappointment with the century.

The first of Leo's attempts at magic.

He first remembers how his use in the diary of the word 'vanquished' resulted in his being quite seriously bullied when he was a new boy at boarding school. He turned the tables on his persecutors with a curse which resulted in a near-fatal accident to the ringleaders. His thoughts and feelings about the people and events of the year 1900 are reawakened.

Comment

There is **irony** (see Literary Terms) in the fact that the grown-up Leo prides himself on his memory but he has suppressed all memories of 1900. We wonder why.

Leo's imagination is shown in the way he considers each drawing in the zodiac.

The episode with Jenkins and Strode is the first time Leo has had to sort out a problem on his own.

His success with the 'spell' means he ceases to be a rather anxious new boy and becomes a popular and respected figure.

The older Leo realises that his younger self understood how to behave in the world of school, but did not understand the world of Brandham Hall.

Our curiosity is also aroused by the fact that Leo seems to blame the events recorded in the diary for so many of his disappointments in life, including the very drab room he is sitting in.

GLOSSARY   **animal, vegetable and mineral** categories of objects in a radio game popular in the 1950s
shot my bolt used up his last means of defending himself
mater and pater public schoolboy terms for mother and father – now very dated

CHAPTER 1

Key experiences before the visit to Norfolk

The story now goes back to 1900.

The first mention of the significance of clothes; a key theme in the novel.

Leo increases his status as a magician (which he cannot explain to his mother) by taking credit for the measles outbreak at school which results in an early finish to the summer term. This second success with spells is beginning to make him feel overconfident.

He is invited to Brandham Hall in Norfolk by Mrs Maudsley, the mother of Marcus, a school acquaintance rather than a friend. He is keen to go, even though he will be away from home for his thirteenth birthday.

Leo's family background has made him less sophisticated than Marcus. Leo is an only child, his father, a local bank manager, has died, and he and his mother are not well off, despite the impressive name of their house, Court Place. Leo was very ill the previous summer and has no lightweight clothes but they agree it is not worth the expense to buy new ones specially for his visit.

COMMENT   Leo's status and popularity at school has been created
through his use of magic. This has had a potentially
dangerous effect on his character, leading him into
thinking that things would go his way 'without much
conscious effort on (his) part' (p. 24).

At this stage in the story, Leo dislikes the heat because
he associates it with being so ill the year before; the
'heat was my enemy' (p. 25).

Leo's sense of his inferior social status between Marcus
and himself is to prove significant later in the story.

GLOSSARY   **Heavenly Bodies** the signs of the zodiac
San (short for sanitarium) the sick bay
Smashem railway schoolboy jokey reference to Chatham railway
the Season the time of the year when fashionable people went
up to London (Town) for a round of balls, parties, concerts,
etc.

CHAPTER 2   Leo arrives at Brandham Hall and is both impressed
and a little intimidated by the size and grandeur of the
First confused house. Leo's first impressions of the Maudsley family
impressions and their guests reflect his age – they all live in a
Leo invents a different world to him and he doesn't really understand
superstition about what they do all day. Mrs Maudsley makes him
the double
staircase.

welcome but Leo finds her daunting. Mr Maudsley seems insignificant in comparison.

He and Marcus are the only children in the house, which is full of young adults, including Marcus's older bother, Denys and his sister, Marion who is, as Marcus points out 'very beautiful' (p. 32). Leo finds the back of the house more interesting than the large formal rooms. He is exploring the outhouses on his own when he discovers a very large deadly nightshade plant – Atropa belladonna – which fascinates him. He decides to tell no-one about it in case it is destroyed.

Marion is linked with the Bella Donna which means beautiful lady in Italian.

COMMENT   Mrs Maudsley seems to dominate the whole household. Leo comments on her intense gaze and dark eyes.

In many ways Marion looks very different from her mother, but she too has a very strong character.

Leo's impressionable nature leads him to accept without question Marcus's comments on his sister's beauty.

This is the first reference to the outhouses and the belladonna plant, both of which will reoccur later in the novel gaining in significance.

GLOSSARY   **Pepys** a famous diary writer of the seventeenth century

seat the main house of an aristocratic family

CHAPTER 3

The problems start

The photograph reflects the differences between Marcus and Leo.

The weather begins to get very hot, and Leo is increasingly uncomfortable in his thick clothes. He feels like an outsider. His clothes are wrong and Marcus lectures him on how to behave. The grown-ups tease him about looking so hot so he tries to pretend the heat is not bothering him. One tea-time he finds himself the centre of attention and feels self-conscious for the first time in his life. He cannot explain his lack of summer clothing or admit to not having any without seeming to blame his mother, and he bursts into tears.

Marion rescues Leo from an embarrassing situation.

Marion offers to take him into Norwich to buy some new clothes because she has realised that he does not have any suitable clothes at home. The family decide his new outfit will be a present from them all. Marion and her mother discuss Marion's waiting until Trimingham arrives but Marion insists on going the next day. Leo does not know who Trimingham is, but starts to feel jealous.

COMMENT

The tea party is an important stage in Leo's growing up. He becomes aware of social inferiority.

He is deeply impressed by Marion's kindness, whereas Mrs Maudsley's comments have, unintentionally, caused him to cry.

The imminent arrival of Trimingham is presented as a significant event but we do not yet know why.

GLOSSARY

Norfolk jacket the name given to a particular style of thick, woollen jacket

knickers long, loose shorts

cad not a gentleman; someone who does not know the proper way to behave

losing face lowering your reputation

bags I the bags bags is slang for trousers and also a word meaning to grab or choose; Denys is making a **pun** (see Literary Terms)

CHAPTER 4

New clothes – new person

Marion and Leo go to Norwich and Leo is extravagantly kitted out. He delights in Marion's attention, though she does leave him for an hour to look round the Cathedral by himself. When he meets her in the square, he glimpses her saying goodbye to someone – a man.

Leo's personality and attitude change.

Leo puts on his new clothes and now he really enjoys being the centre of attention at tea-time. He feels like a different person, a valued member of the family. No longer distressed by the heat, he hopes the weather will get even hotter.

A swimming expedition is arranged, but Leo is waiting for his mother's permission to swim and goes as an observer. On the walk to the river, Marcus explains about Trimingham's war-scarred face and that Mrs Maudsley wants Marion to marry him. Leo is even more confused about Trimingham's social status.

Leo is increasingly attracted to Marion.   A neighbouring farmer, Ted Burgess, is already in the water. Because he is a tenant of Trimingham's, the group wait for him to have one last swim. Leo is impressed by his muscular body and feels a little afraid of him as well. Ted leaves in a hurry when he hears the sound of Marion's voice complaining that her hair has got wet. Leo has brought his swimming costume even though he cannot swim and has begun to feel awkward as a result. He suggests that Marion should drape it round her shoulders to help dry her wet hair and once again feels he is important.

COMMENT   This chapter shows us further developments in Leo's character:

- Marion makes him feel special and in his imagination he links her to the virgin in his zodiac.
- He no longer feels like an outsider.
- His attitude to the hot weather has changed.
- His identification with the water carrier of the zodiac has found a real life example in Ted Burgess.
- He has unthinkingly lied for Marion when she says they met no-one.

Denys's patronising way of talking about Ted reminds us of the importance of class distinctions in late-Victorian England.

GLOSSARY **sovereigns and guineas** gold coins

bathing-suit (also **bathing dress**) old-fashioned forms of swimwear

not even a Mr someone of a lower social class who could be addressed by his surname only

CHAPTERS 5—6

Trimingham makes an impact

Next day, Marcus is not feeling well and stays in bed. Despite Marcus's warning, Leo is shocked by his first sight of Trimingham's face but notices how much attention Mrs Maudsley pays to him.

Marion keeps Leo company on the walk to church. Although Trimingham overtakes them, he does not join them. During the service, Leo reads the memorials to the family in the church and realises the ninth Viscount Trimingham is still alive, though he is confused by the absence of any reference to a fifth viscount. He also tries to sort out his own ideas about what is right and wrong, good and bad.

Leo begins to act as a go-between.

As he walks back to the Hall alone, he is joined by Trimingham and realises who he really is. Trimingham (or Hugh) tactfully rescues Leo from further embarrassment about how to refer to him. He asks Leo to run on ahead with a message to Marion who finds it difficult to understand his pronunciation of 'Hugh'. Leo thinks Hugh is disappointed when he brings him Marion's message of thanks for finding her prayer book. Meanwhile the doctor has visited Marcus and Leo has been moved out as a precaution against infection. He now has a room all to himself and feels this marks a new stage in his life at Brandham Hall which he celebrates by changing into his new clothes.

COMMENT

Leo's innocence is shown when he has to ask Marion if her hair 'only comes down by accident' and his confusion about how to address Trimingham once he knows he is a Lord.

The theme of class-consciousness is developed through Leo's abrupt change of attitude to Trimingham when he understands his social status.

The schoolboy slang used by Leo and Marcus when they are alone together reminds us of the fact they are much younger than the others and links back to an environment in which Leo knew what the rules were and how to behave.

Leo is now on his own.

GLOSSARY   **fast** rather daring or unconventional
                   lesson the Bible reading
                   Collect and **Litany** parts of the church service

Identify the speaker.

1 'Are you vanquished, Colston, are you vanquished?'

Identify the person 'to whom' this comment refers.

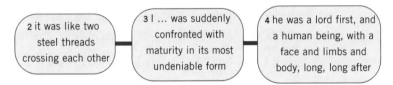

2 it was like two steel threads crossing each other

3 I ... was suddenly confronted with maturity in its most undeniable form

4 he was a lord first, and a human being, with a face and limbs and body, long, long after

Identify 'when' this occurs.

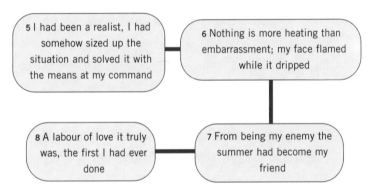

5 I had been a realist, I had somehow sized up the situation and solved it with the means at my command

6 Nothing is more heating than embarrassment; my face flamed while it dripped

8 A labour of love it truly was, the first I had ever done

7 From being my enemy the summer had become my friend

Check your answers on page 82.

B *Consider these issues.*

a The importance of Leo's home background.

b The significance of the events at school.

c The reasons for Leo's fascination with the signs of the zodiac.

d The ways in which L.P. Hartley shows the differences in social status between Leo and his hosts.

e The importance of clothes.

Part two

CHAPTER 7

Meeting with Ted Burgess

Leo has become very self-important and elated by both the heat and his treatment by what he sees as his superiors. Leo feels he has joined the celestial bodies of the zodiac. Left to explore by himself, and now feeling liberated rather than oppressed by the heat, Leo wanders back to the sluice-gate and the river, noticing how the heat is beginning to dry everything up. He eventually ends up in a farmyard where he feels almost obliged to slide down the haystack but forgets to check if it is safe to do so. The yell he lets out when he gashes his knee alerts Ted Burgess, whose farm it is. His initial anger is calmed when he realises that Leo is staying at the Hall.

Leo consciously behaves in the way he thinks people expect him to.

In return for Ted's kindness in bandaging his knee (and also because Ted compliments him on his bravery) Leo asks if there is anything he can do. Before answering, Ted takes Leo to see the horses, which he isn't much interested in, and is confused by Ted's calling his favourite horse, 'wild oats'. After much hesitation and questioning about Leo's relationship with Marion and his circumstances at the Hall, Ted asks him to take a 'business' letter to her, first swearing him to secrecy. Leo is delighted and intrigued. Ted offers Leo free use of his haystack

Leo starts to act as a go-between for Ted and Marion.

When he arrives back at the house, Marion offers to rebandage his knee. Leo notices, but does not understand, her agitation when he eventually remembers to give her the letter, and she too swears him to secrecy.

COMMENT

Ted and Leo are alike in that they both change their behaviour when speaking to someone they see as socially superior.

Leo shows that he does not understand the grown-up feelings and attitudes of the people he is acting for. He is a boy in an adult world.

The grown-up Leo comments that by this stage in the story he had begun to confuse reality and the world of his imagination.

GLOSSARY   **Spartan** a brave, tough person

wild oats a reference to 'sowing wild oats' meaning youthful indiscretions

catechism a series of questions and answers (originally religious)

blue-lined writing paper lined writing paper was considered lower class

the place where you pull the chain a euphemism for the toilet or WC

CHAPTER 8

Alone in a grown-up world

Leo senses the tension in the air since Trimingham's arrival. Even Mrs Maudsley seems to consult him when making arrangements for the day's activities.

As Marcus is still unwell, Leo goes out with the adults. At a picnic, Trimingham praises him to Marion, calling him Mercury. At first Leo thinks this is a reference to his small size, but he is overjoyed when Trimingham tells him that Mercury was the messenger of the gods.

Later, half asleep, Leo overhears Marion suggesting that he must be bored and would be happier left behind

Note the growing tension between Marion and her mother.

at the house. Mrs Maudsley calls him Marion's 'little lamb' because of his devotion to her. Mrs Maudsley reacts strongly to Marion's suggesting that the ball (at which her engagement to Trimingham will be announced) may have to be put off if Marcus really has got measles. Leo realises he admires and trusts Trimingham.

Leo is confused by adult phraseology.

On the journey home, Leo rides beside the coachman, whose factual conversation he enjoys much more than the usual adult talk, though he does not understand why the coachman refers to Ted as 'a bit of a lad'. There is a letter from his mother waiting for him on his return, and Leo suddenly realises how far away and different this world seems from his home. Having written his reply, Leo rushes to see what the maximum temperature has been that day. He is delighted to find how hot it was (Mr Maudsley thinks it may be a record) but wants the temperature to go even higher.

Trimingham spots Leo and asks him to find Marion for a game of croquet. He meets her coming along the path from the outhouses. After some confusion caused by Leo's pronunciation of 'Hugh', he gives her the message and is surprised by her lack of enthusiasm. She lies to him, saying that her mother is afraid he will be bored by tomorrow's visit and that he might like to stay behind. She turns the conversation to Leo, asking how he will spend his time and he finds himself being asked

Leo is now involved in taking messages between all three central characters.

to take a letter to Ted Burgess. Leo, at her prompting, tells her that he likes Ted, but he also explains that he likes Trimingham better, and not simply because he has a title. Emboldened, he also confesses that he is eager to take the message because he likes her too. Marion is tempted not to go to play croquet, but seeing Leo's disappointment, changes her mind.

COMMENT   Now he has been called Mercury, Leo has, in his
           imagination, linked himself with the god-like characters
           of the zodiac, but also with the rising mercury in the
           thermometer.

           He cannot bring himself to be critical of Marion, even
           when she tells him a lie.

           Leo cannot understand the tension in the situation
           between Marion and her mother, or between Marion
           and Trimingham, any more than he can guess at the
           relationship between Ted and Marion.

           Leo's role as a go-between is confirmed.

GLOSSARY   **ha-ha** concealed ditch separating the formal part of the garden
           from the grounds beyond

           dead ground a military term referring to an area out of the firing
           line

CHAPTERS 9–10

Leo discovers   Leo continues to carry messages between Marion and
romantic love   Ted. On one occasion he finds Ted in the cornfield
Note the   where he has been shooting rabbits and is horrified
premonition of   when a smear of blood appears on the letter Ted has
Ted's fate.   just been given. He also thinks of Ted as the last sheaf
                       of corn the harvesters will come back to cut down. He
                       enjoys sliding down the haystack, which also offers him
                       as excuse for his visit. Leo speculates on what the notes
                       might be about, but his imagination cannot guess at the
                       truth, except that he senses how important they are to
                       Marion.

                       Marcus has now recovered from his illness and Leo
                       immediately realises, to his great disappointment, that
                       he will not be able to escape Marcus's company to take
                       the messages. Before he can explain his problem to
                       Marion, she pushes a letter in to his hand just as they

are joined by Trimingham. Leo contrives to leave Marcus behind while he goes on his errand. Leo's lack of understanding of courtship and sex makes it impossible for him to imagine Marion in a romantic situation, though Marcus gives him a broad hint. On the way to Ted's farm Leo realises that, in her haste, Marion has not sealed the envelope. Wrestling with his conscience, Leo compromises by only looking at the words he can see without taking the letter out of the envelope. The loving words he can see are enough to both horrify and disappoint him. He cannot believe how blind he has been and is devastated that Marion should be involved in something he thinks is as ridiculous as 'spooning'.

Leo's curiosity gets the better of him.

Nevertheless, he must take the letter and as he walks on he notices the devastation brought about by the heat. The river is almost dried up. He begins to think less harshly of Marion, telling himself that if Marion can fall in love, it cannot be so silly after all, though he is less happy about her being in love with Ted who is only a farmer. But when he reaches the farm he cannot help but be impressed by Ted's physique, and cannot imagine that he too would be involved in anything 'silly'.

Leo's emotions are in turmoil.

When Leo explains that he cannot take messages anymore, Ted tells him how upset Marion will be. In answer to Leo's question about how they managed before he came, Ted awkwardly tries to explain something of their feelings and emotions, but Leo feels increasingly bewildered and upset. He is even more confused when Ted, explaining that he was not in the fields because he has been looking after a pregnant mare, describes what caused her condition as 'spooning'. He tries, not very successfully, to explain something of the facts of life, and, despite his ignorance, Leo suddenly realises that love and sex are a natural part of

Ted tries emotional blackmail.

life. Ted is reluctant to go further in his explanations, but in response to Leo's pestering, promises to tell him about 'spooning' if he will continue to take messages. However, Ted did not need to pressurise him into promising to continue as 'postman'; Leo realises how much it means to him as well as to them.

COMMENT   Marcus, despite being a year younger, is more sophisticated and aware of the grown-up world than Leo who, in contrast, is naïve and ignorant of sex.

Leo's tendency to apply 'school rules' to the outside world shows in the way he convinces himself that it is OK to read part of the letter.

Leo's feelings about Ted in this section of the novel have clear links with his first impressions in Chapter 4. This is also the first time he sees Ted handling his shotgun.

At the end of this visit, Leo's growing maturity makes him less enthusiastic about sliding down the haystack.

GLOSSARY   **Lord Roberts, Kitchener, Kruger, de Wet** military commanders on both sides of the Boer War being fought in South Africa
Stanley and Livingstone when Stanley found Livingstone in the African jungle, his famous greeting was 'Doctor Livingstone, I presume?'
spooning courting; silly or sentimental love-making
Eleventh Commandment 'do not get found out'. There are Ten Commandments in the Bible
sell deception, let down
old fashioned mature beyond your years, perceptive (when applied to children)

A *Identify the person 'to whom' this comment refers.*

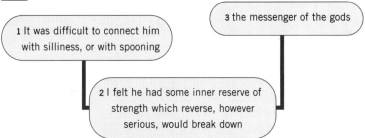

1 It was difficult to connect him with silliness, or with spooning

3 the messenger of the gods

2 I felt he had some inner reserve of strength which reverse, however serious, would break down

'Who to' or 'when' does this happen.

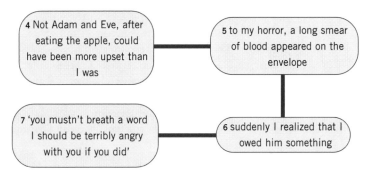

4 Not Adam and Eve, after eating the apple, could have been more upset than I was

5 to my horror, a long smear of blood appeared on the envelope

7 'you mustn't breath a word I should be terribly angry with you if you did'

6 suddenly I realized that I owed him something

Check your answers on page 82.

B *Consider these issues.*

a Leo's reasons for becoming a 'go-between'.

b Leo's attitude and feelings towards i)Ted and ii)Trimingham and how they differ.

c The way the heat is described as affecting the landscape and how this relates to the developing emotional climate.

d The ways in which L.P. Hartley shows Leo's sexual and emotional naïvety.

PART THREE

CHAPTERS 11–12

Leo's moment of glory

Leo is delighted to be included as twelfth man in the annual cricket match between the Hall and the village and his happiness is increased by Marion's suggesting he extend his visit by a week. When Marion sends him with an unkind reply to Trimingham's request for a song at the cricket supper, Leo modifies the message to spare his feelings and then misreports the reaction to Marion, who seems annoyed.

Leo starts to 'edit' the messages.

The village team wears a variety of clothes and Leo is convinced that the immaculately dressed team from the Hall must win. Indeed he is desperately anxious that they do, even though Ted is playing for the village. **Ironically** (see Literary Terms), when Trimingham 'introduces' Leo to Ted, he recommends him as a messenger. Despite Leo's hero-worship, Trimingham does not make a high score (though he bats elegantly) and is satirically applauded by Marion. Wickets continue to fall but Mr Maudsley, a most unlikely cricketer in Leo's eyes, saves the day, by careful batting and good judgement.

Further evidence of strain between Marion and Trimingham is provided.

When Ted goes out to bat, Leo experiences divided loyalties. On the one hand, Ted plays a flamboyant, if chancy innings and Leo hopes he will make a high score. But on the other hand, the idea of the village winning upsets his rigid ideas of social class. Marion too seems very excited by the prospect of Ted's success and Leo realises that the contest on the cricket field is partly over her, as well as representing other conflicts and tensions between social classes.

The match becomes an omen for the future.

Suddenly a player is injured and Leo has to act as a substitute fielder. No longer able to sit on the sidelines, he must participate in the game. At first he is very nervous, and takes refuge in what he sees as the safety of a 'fairy ring' (p. 125), but he soon becomes absorbed in the game.

The match reaches crisis point, and Trimingham bowls to Ted. Leo sees the ball flying towards him and before he can think, he has caught it. His delight in the congratulations is mixed with a real sense of regret. He feels he must at least apologise to Ted, explaining that he 'didn't really mean to catch (him) out' (p. 128).

Leo and Marcus bicker in school boy language about how Leo's catch should be recorded on the score card.

COMMENT   The events of the cricket match and Leo's part in it reflect or foretell many key ideas and events in the novel. The description of the match, and the concert which follows, need to be read carefully.

The imminent changes in British society are also hinted at:
- The near-defeat of the Hall echoes the near-defeat of the British in South Africa fighting the Boers, who were not thought to be 'gentlemen'.
- Ted, a tenant, bats more successfully than his landlord, Trimingham, although Trimingham does eventually get Ted out.
- Money, in the form of Mr Maudsley, the banker, helps the Hall to win.

The weather is again used to reflect feelings and mood; Leo notices a large cloud hanging over the ground – 'A creation of the heat' (p. 122).

Leo once more finds 'safety' in some form of magic.

GLOSSARY   **twelfth man** an extra member of the team in case a team member is injured

nailer clever or skilled person

late cuts a way of batting

hosts of Midian the enemy

fairy ring circle of darker grass caused by fungus and thought to
keep safe the person standing inside it – a superstition

CHAPTER 13

Village versus
Hall
continued

A supper follows the cricket match. After Mr Maudsley
has made a very fluent speech (much to Leo's surprise)
an informal concert is due to take place. As the pianist
is unable to come, Marion offers to act as accompanist
and shows her considerable skill. When his turn arrives,
Ted shows a marked reluctance to sing, even though he
has brought his music with him. When Ted and
Marion are acknowledging the applause, one of the
villagers wonders why Ted is suddenly so shy and goes
on to comment what a handsome couple they make 'If
it wasn't for the difference' (p. 134) in their social
status.

For the second
time in one day,
Leo successfully
copes with being
the centre of
attention.

After sitting back and enjoying the music, Leo suddenly
finds himself being asked to sing. He is at first horrified
because he has no music with him, but Marion knows
the music by heart. Leo's second song is a sacred one.
He sings it beautifully but, although he and Marion
receive loud applause, it seems to mark the end of the
evening, which Marion closes by singing 'Home, Sweet

Home' (as Trimingham had requested). Leo's adoration of Marion reaches new heights.

On the walk back to the Hall, Marcus complains about the smell of the villagers at the supper, and teases Leo about his singing, though he also tells him how Trimingham praised him to Mrs Maudsley. Finally, he explains that Marion has agreed to marry Trimingham and their engagement will be announced after the forthcoming ball. Leo is pleased.

COMMENT   Their appearance at supper further contrasts Ted and Trimingham. Ted is ill at ease in a formal suit which constricts his naturalness and muscular body.

The sentimental songs chosen affect Leo emotionally, but he cannot really understand the passions being expressed.

Marion once again saves Leo from an embarrassing situation. (Look back at the tea party scene in Chapter 3.)

Leo has now twice in one day coped with the demands of the adult world, but the older Leo warns us in this chapter that he was not successful on the third occasion.

GLOSSARY   **dovetailed** sitting alternately

dog-eared turned down the corner (to make it easier to turn the page quickly)

music of the spheres the imaginary music made by the planets as they revolve

goosy come out in goose pimples; shivery

plebs short for plebians, the common people in ancient Rome

CHAPTERS 14–15

Leo's life becomes more comlicated   The following day, Leo continues to feel elated; he has won the cricket match, he has made the concert a

Leo is still very naïve in his understanding of adult relationships.

success. Marion's forthcoming engagement means that his 'two idols' will be united. He assumes he will no longer be needed to take messages (another possible problem solved) as it does not occur to him that Marion will continue her relationship with Ted. He assumes she must share his hero-worship of Trimingham, especially as she will also become mistress of Brandham Hall. He tries to evaluate his mixed feelings about ceasing to be the 'postman' and his combination of admiration and jealousy for Ted. The older Leo thinks back and realises that he took satisfaction from having twice outshone Ted, on the cricket field and in the concert. Leo attempts to communicate his feelings of elation in a letter to his mother asking for permission to stay on another week.

Leo learns of the fate of the fifth viscount.

During the church service, Leo amuses himself by rereading the memorials to the Triminghams, adding Marion's name to those of the viscountesses. He is not jealous at the thought of the marriage to a viscount whereas he sees Ted as some kind of rival. He is still puzzled by the absence of reference to the fifth viscount and asks Trimingham about it on the way home. Trimingham patiently explains to him the story of his death abroad in a duel over his wife. Leo begins to draw a parallel between Trimingham's situation and his ancestor's, particularly when Trimingham admits that men do still occasionally shoot each other over a woman, although duelling is illegal. He insists, however, that 'Nothing is ever a lady's fault' (p. 149).

These are new and surprising ideas to Leo, who is still turning them over in his mind, together with the prospect of Marion's imminent rise in social status, when Marion asks him to take a letter to Ted. Horrified, Leo immediately assumes that such a situation might lead to murder. He desperately tries to explain that he cannot take the letter but his usual trouble in pronouncing Hugh frustrates him. When he blurts out that Hugh might be upset, Marion's temper erupts. She accuses Leo of ingratitude and then of being mercenary, calling him 'a little Shylock' (p. 154), a reference he does not understand, so he cannot deny it. Leo takes the letter and runs. He is deeply hurt by Marion's treatment of him. He thought she had made him into someone special because she really liked him. Now he thinks she was only kind to him because he could be useful and that all his precious memories are based on illusion and deceit.

Leo sees Marion in a new light.

As he crosses the sluice, he begins to calm down and notices the devastation the drought is causing. He still feels that Marion has simply been exploiting him from the very start of his visit but as this does not fit in with Trimingham's comment that 'Nothing is ever a lady's fault', he transfers the blame onto Ted. On reaching the farm he is reluctant to go inside where he finds Ted cleaning his gun. Ted's sympathy over his tear-stained face causes Leo to cry even more and Ted anxiously tries to find something to cheer him up. Leo watches Ted shooting rooks with some skill and then helps him clean the gun. He is thrilled to be allowed to handle the gun though Ted tells him off for pointing it at him. While Ted makes some tea, Leo oils his cricket bat for him and begins to feel calmer. Eventually Ted guesses that it was Marion who made Leo cry and, realising something of the strain Leo has been under, but also wanting him to continue as postman, asks if there is any way he can reward Leo. Tempted to say 'nothing' (p. 162), Leo suddenly remembers Ted's promise to explain about 'spooning'. Ted does his awkward best but Leo continues to pester him until his temper snaps and he orders Leo out of the house.

The gun episode is another hint about what will happen in the future.

COMMENT   Leo's feelings towards both Marion and Ted become very confused. He sees their illtempers, and both use emotional blackmail and threats towards him. As readers, we are able to see and understand the strain that Marion and Ted are suffering in a way that the young Leo cannot.

The story of the fifth viscount makes a deep impression on Leo, and is important in influencing his later thoughts and behaviour.

L.P. Hartley continues to use the effect of the heat on the landscape as a **metaphor** (see Literary Terms) for the ultimately destructive relationships which are developing.

We are shown Ted handling his gun, and see how closely Leo links the two in his imagination.

GLOSSARY **Shylock** a character in Shakespeare known for his love of money – a very mean person

put-up job a deliberately contrived situation, a confidence trick

LRAM an academic music qualification

CHAPTERS 16–17

Leo wants to escape

At tea-time, Mrs Maudsley is unwell and Marion has taken her mother's place. Trimingham sits beside her, and Leo realises this is what the scene will be like after they are married. Leo's hurt feelings are partially soothed by the fuss everyone makes of him, but he ignores Marion's look, and hides away in his room.

The strain is taking its toll on Leo and Mrs Maudsley.

Leo writes another letter home, begging his mother to rescue him from what he now feels to be an intolerable situation, though he cannot tell her the full extent or cause of his unhappiness. Leo feels that the relationship between Marion and Ted is somehow his fault, and that if he goes away, even though he doesn't want to leave, the crisis will be averted. On his way back from the postbox, he meets Trimingham who asks him to find Marion and who is a bit taken aback by Leo's apparent reluctance. Leo then remembers that Marion has said she was going to visit her old nanny. Trimingham laughingly explains that the visit will be a waste of time because Marion says Nanny Robson is so forgetful.

Marcus is much more sophisticated than Leo.

On his way to explore the rubbish heap, Leo meets Marcus, and they talk in their special mixture of real and schoolboy French. Leo is less fluent than Marcus and has to work hard to compete. They find a footprint and Leo remembers that the only adult he has ever met on this path is Marion but he says nothing. Marcus explains that his mother has a very anxious disposition and is ill, worrying whether Marion will keep to her engagement. Marcus also discounts any suggestion that Nanny Robson is getting forgetful. He explains that one of the reasons for Marion's trip to London is to buy Leo's birthday present – a bicycle (a rare and expensive item at this time.) Leo's delight is spoiled when Marcus adds that it will be a green bicycle because Marion

Leo sees his new clothes in a different light.

thinks Leo is green (i.e. naïve and foolish). Leo does not realise that Marcus is not telling the truth, and is deeply hurt. He thinks that Marion has been making fun of him from the beginning when she chose the green suit. He retaliates by boasting in French that he

Leo almost betrays Marion.

knows where Marion really is (although he doesn't), forgetting that Marcus will tell tales to his mother.

When they reach the outhouses, Leo is both frightened and fascinated by the astonishing way the belladonna plant has grown. Unlike everything else, it has flourished in the heat. The boys are still staring at it when they hear voices nearby. Leo immediately

Leo acts quickly to protect Marion and Ted.

recognises Ted's voice but when Marcus suggests they disturb what he thinks is a courting couple, Leo has the presence of mind to dismiss the suggestion as 'boring' – a word which Marcus himself uses as a criticism. They leave, but Leo cannot persuade Marcus not to tell his mother. On the way back, Leo is tempted by further thoughts of the bicycle, and even goes as far as taking his letter out of the postbox. He finally decides to send it as he feels the bicycle might also be intended as a bribe or trap.

COMMENT   The text of Leo's letter home shows just how young he is and the difficulty he has in expressing his feelings about being involved in such a grown-up situation.

We see the very uneasy nature of his 'friendship' with Marcus. At times, there is even a kind of hostility between them which makes Leo seem even more isolated and lonely.

The strain of waiting for the announcement of the engagement seems to be affecting everyone.

We learn for the first time of Mrs Maudsley's very weak nerves; she is what Marcus calls 'un peu hystérique' (a bit hysterical – p. 173) – a hint of her future behaviour.

L.P. Hartley again links Leo's feelings about the belladonna plant with his relationship with Marion (and the adult world of sex and romance).

Leo may have told Marcus more than he realises about his involvement in the Ted / Marion situation.

GLOSSARY   *amour propre* pride, self-esteem (French)
hush-money money given in return for keeping quiet about something, a bribe

A *'To what' event does this refer to.*

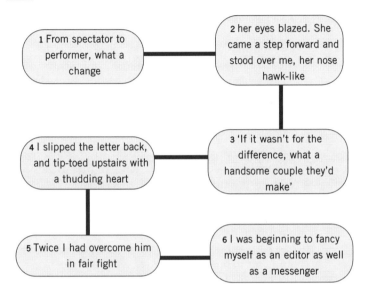

1 From spectator to performer, what a change

2 her eyes blazed. She came a step forward and stood over me, her nose hawk-like

4 I slipped the letter back, and tip-toed upstairs with a thudding heart

3 'If it wasn't for the difference, what a handsome couple they'd make'

5 Twice I had overcome him in fair fight

6 I was beginning to fancy myself as an editor as well as a messenger

Check your answers on page 82.

B *Consider these issues.*

a The ways in which the cricket match and the concert are key episodes in the novel.

b Why the story of the fifth viscount has such an impact on Leo.

c Marion's behaviour in the light of Trimingham's comment that 'Nothing is ever a lady's fault'.

d The way Hartley shows us the changing stages of Leo's state of mind in this section; from growing confidence to triumph and elation then hurt, confusion and despair.

PART FOUR

CHAPTER 18

Ted Burgess's reputation is discussed

The next morning both Marion and her mother are absent from the breakfast table; Marion has gone to London and Mrs Maudsley is still ill. Leo tries to reassess his feelings about them both and their relationship with each other. Leo has had his feelings of love and admiration for Marion poisoned by Marcus's saying she thought of him as green and it never occurs to him that Marcus was lying.

Leo is still a boy in an adult situation.

After breakfast, Marcus patronises Leo by telling him a joke which he does not understand. In Mrs Maudsley's absence, the atmosphere is more relaxed and Leo feels happier because he is also not under any pressure from Marion. He receives a letter of apology from Ted offering to try again to explain the facts of life to him. Leo is almost convinced by its sincerity, though it does not occur to him that it needs a reply. Trimingham describes Ted as a bit of a 'lady killer' (p. 188) – another phrase which Leo does not understand, but he thinks that because he will be leaving shortly, there is no danger of the situation ending in bloodshed. Leo has been encouraged by Ted and Marion to think he is vitally important to their relationship, and so is convinced that if he leaves, Marion will marry Trimingham and everything will be all right.

Trimingham also explains what 'getting your rag out' (p. 189) means, a phrase used by Ted in his letter.

We learn more about Ted's reputation in the area.

When Mr Maudsley joins in the conversation, we learn that Trimingham has been trying to persuade Ted to volunteer to join the Army, particularly as he is a good shot. He was originally reluctant, but he now seems more likely to join up. Mr Maudsley comments that, given his reputation with the ladies, Ted won't be a loss to the district, adding that he has heard that Ted has 'got a woman' (p. 191) in the vicinity of the Hall, having been seen recently in the grounds. Leo feels uncomfortable listening to this talk (though he thinks the reference to a woman is the lady who cleans for him) as he also feels uncomfortable when the slightly erotic paintings are pointed out to him.

COMMENT   Ted's letter gives us his version of events to balance out Leo's account.

The conversation between Mr Maudsley and Trimingham suggests that Ted and Marion's relationship is in danger of discovery.

The fact that Ted is considering volunteering for the army shows he too is feeling the strain and wants to be out of the way if Marion marries Trimingham.

Leo is yet again confused by adult language, which he takes literally and is presented as a child in an adult world.

GLOSSARY   **lady-killer** deliberately attractive to women
have a crack at give something a try
daily woman someone who comes in each day to clean the house, etc.

CHAPTERS 19–20

Everything   Leo is waiting for his mother to recall him home, but
starts to go   still listens with interest to Marcus's descriptions of the
wrong   preparations for the forthcoming ball and Leo's birthday party. Despite his hurt feelings, he begins to feel some regret at missing all the excitement and presents. Marion is scheduled to make a dramatic appearance riding the birthday bicycle.

No telegram or letter has arrived from Leo's mother but he is still convinced that he will be leaving shortly. He feels he should say goodbye to Ted and manages to escape from Marcus by pretending Ted has offered to teach him to swim.

Leo volunteers to act as go-between again.

When he meets Ted harvesting the last of his corn, he is surprised to see how he has aged and lost weight. When Leo asks him if he is going to war because Marion is engaged to Trimingham, Ted reveals that it all depends on Marion. He awkwardly tries to apologise to Leo for involving him in the situation, even addressing him politely as Master Colston. As he is leaving, Leo offers to take one last message, just to show he is still friends with Ted, and thinking that he will be back home when the message takes effect. Ted is grateful and sends an oral message.

Leo cannot escape.

Arriving back at the Hall, Leo finds a letter waiting for him from his mother. Filled with relief, he opens it to find that she has been confused by receiving two contradictory letters from him and feels he should stay for the extended visit. Leo is devastated. In a confused way he realises that somehow his relationship with Marion has caused all the turmoil he now experiences. He feels he knows how to cope with Ted and his anger or threats, but he is helpless against Marion's charms. He decides he must try to stay away from her but knows that will only postpone the inevitable crisis.

Leo tries to influence events but forgets that he may have to suffer the consequences.

Mrs Maudsley has recovered, and the atmosphere at breakfast the next day is tense once more. Marion catches up with Leo, and offers him a kind of apology for her behaviour before she left for London. Leo finally realises how unhappy she is. Her reference to hard beds reminds Leo of both Trimingham as a former soldier and Ted as a prospective one. After the usual confusion caused by Leo's pronunciation of Hugh, Marion is astonished and angry to discover that Ted has been approached to volunteer as a soldier. She furiously denounces Trimingham's behaviour as blackmail and is determined to prevent Ted from enlisting. Terrified by her reactions and remembering the fate of the fifth viscount, Leo explains that Trimingham does not know about the messages but is patriotically trying to recruit soldiers. When he suggests that Ted might want to go to fight, Marion's anguish is clear and Leo understands how much she cares for Ted. Marion is caught between her love for Ted, and her need to make a suitable marriage. We are also given an insight into Marion's dilemma and the pressures of class distinction; she loves Ted but realises that marriage to a farmer is socially impossible. Her family expect her to marry into the aristocracy.

New light is Shed on Marion's character and stituation.

When she finally bursts into tears, all Leo's hurt and resentment melts away and he once more sees her as his ideal woman. In response to her inquiry, Leo passes on Ted's message, but changes the time from six thirty to six o'clock on Friday. He has remembered his plan to foil a further meeting between the lovers, but in the emotion of the moment, he has forgotten he originally thought he would be at home by Friday. Both he and Marion have forgotten that Leo's birthday will be celebrated at that time.

COMMENT

Leo is torn between wanting to escape from the ever-increasing tension and wanting to experience the excitement of the ball and the coveted present of the bicycle.

We are reminded of Mrs Colston's character by the contents of her letter.

L.P. Hartley uses Ted's appearance to show the strain he is under.

The differences in the way that Ted and Marion offer their apologies to Leo reveal some differences in their character, which are further shown in the contrast between Marion's decisiveness and Ted's willingness to let Marion decide whether or not he should join the army.

The key role Marion plays in the lives of both Leo and Ted is made plain here.

Leo's alteration of the time in the message increases the tension; it seems more and more likely Marion and Ted's relationship will be discovered.

GLOSSARY **fast** not quite respectable, daring
façon de parler a way of speaking (French)
Jingo a particularly patriotic person

CHAPTERS 21–22

Magic and the belladonna plant

Although Leo is pleased that he feels close to Marion once more, he is still very worried about the implications of the situation between Trimingham, Marion and Ted. The fate of the fifth viscount haunts

Leo appreciates the fact that Ted has treated him as a real person but is very confused about where his loyalties lie.

him, he hates to see Marion so unhappy, but he discovers that his deepest feelings of concern are about Ted, partly because he thinks that Ted has treated him as something more than a pet or errand boy. He struggles to work out the morality of the situation, and because he cannot bring himself to blame either Marion or Trimingham, he ends up blaming Ted. Having already falsified the message, he hopes that Ted and Marion will fall out if he keeps her waiting.

Once again Leo thinks he can control events.

The more he thinks, the more he becomes convinced that the Marion–Ted relationship must come to an end because it has overshadowed and spoilt everything else that might have made Leo's visit so wonderful. In desperation he turns to magic to solve his problems just as he did at school, though he does not want to harm anyone, only break what he thinks of as Ted's spell over Marion.

That evening he slips out of the house after bedtime, though his nerve almost fails as he crosses the hall. He has chosen the belladonna plant as the raw material of his spell because it is so poisonous and he has prepared the whole episode of casting his spell like a chemistry experiment at school. When he arrives at the outhouse to collect samples of the plant, he is taken aback by the powerful feelings it arouses in him. He forces himself into the midst of the plant, but soon finds himself lashing out at it in a desperate panic to escape. Finally it is uprooted and destroyed.

His birthday marks a change in Leo's attitude to life.

The morning after he has cast his spell, Leo feels more confident, especially as the heat wave also seems to be over and rain is forecast. It is his thirteenth birthday and Leo feels that he must put aside his childish fantasies and behave in a more grown-up way. He contrasts himself unfavourably with Marcus who is interested in what is going on around him, not in an imaginary world. He thinks of all his experiences at Brandham as happening to another boy and he partly blames the adults for indulging his fantasies, as well as Marion for flattering his self-importance. He instinctively links the extraordinary events with the extraordinary weather. To mark what he regards as a return to normality, he puts on his Norfolk suit because his green outfit represents his make-believe self.

At breakfast he is the centre of attention which he now enjoys. Trimingham courteously spares Leo embarrassment by trying on his aunt's present of a tie which Marcus later explains it would not be acceptable for Leo to wear.

Now he has decided to be practical and sensible, Leo finds his birthday rather dull. Realising he has imposed too big a burden on himself, he changes his clothes to symbolise a return to his freer, imaginative self.

COMMENT   The **symbolic** (see Literary Terms) link hinted at in earlier stages of the story between the Ted–Marion relationship, Leo and the belladonna plant is now made clear.

These two chapters show Leo struggling to reconcile the world of his imagination with the real world; he goes from the fantasy world of his spell, to the world of facts and common sense, and then back to his 'new' self in green.

Once again clothes are important ways of representing feelings as well as social status.

There are echoes here of the earlier tea party scenes in the novel but this time Leo does not feel awkward.

Leo's feelings about the other central characters and their relationship to him are explored but he does not realise the element of jealousy in his attitude to Ted.

At the end of Chapter 22, Leo thinks the **catastrophe** (see Literary Terms) he feared has been avoided, but we as readers understand that this is not so, and wait for the **denouement** (see Literary Terms).

GLOSSARY   **Jaeger** name of a shop specialising at this time in pure wool clothing

Delenda est belladonna the belladonna must be destroyed; a reference to a famous phrase in Latin

having a field day really enjoying yourself, letting yourself go

Liverpool Street a London railway station; Marion thinks of Leo as being labeled like a parcel to be sent by train

cad not a gentleman

CHAPTER 23

The final
catastrophe

The weather
reflects the
approaching crisis.

There is a storm brewing and Leo's birthday picnic
looks increasingly unlikely, Marion asks Leo to take a
message, but their noisy conversation attracts the
attention of Mrs Maudsley who also sees the letter,
dropped by Leo. She invites Leo to walk with her in
the garden. He starts to tell her about the belladonna
plant, but changes his mind. He does, however,
mention the outhouses.

Marion had pretended that the letter was for Nanny
Robson, but Mrs Maudsley is suspicious and calls Leo's
bluff. In desperation he pretends to have lost the letter,
and she tries to pressurise him into telling her where he
has taken the other letters. Leo is desperate, but is
rescued by the storm suddenly breaking, and they both
have to rush indoors. Leo's sense of being under threat
is increased when he finds his room being prepared for
another guest.

At tea-time, waiting for Mrs Maudsley to appear, Leo
is frightened she will continue to question him, but she
is kind and shows him his special cake.

The sense of
tension increases.

Marion is late arriving and the carriage is sent for her.
The birthday tea continues, but the conversation is
stilted. Despite the crackers, the cake and the bicycle,
this is not the special birthday Leo had been looking
forward to. The butler announces that Marion has not
been to Nanny Robson's, and suddenly Mrs Maudsley
tells Leo to show her where she is. As he follows her
out of the house, even his new bicycle waiting in the
hall has a grotesque look, and he quickly find himself
running to catch up with Mrs Maudsley as she marches
along the cinder path.

Leo finally sees
what 'spooning' is.

He desperately tries to misdirect her, but she seems
instinctively to make for the outhouse containing the

belladonna. Leo is forced to join her looking through the doorway, to see Marion and Ted making love. Mrs Maudsley screams hysterically, and Leo remembers nothing more, except that Ted went home and shot himself.

COMMENT   L.P. Hartley brings together many of the strands of the story together at this climax of the action:
- Leo as a go-between and his involvement in adult relationships
- The final discovery of the doomed love of Marion and Ted
- The weather reflecting the emotional climate
- The birthday party and Leo once again being the centre of attraction
- Ted's death by his own shotgun
- The belladonna and Leo's curiosity about sex

GLOSSARY   **cavalier** admirer, a willing servant
brougham a kind of carriage

A *Identify the person 'to whom' this comment refers.*

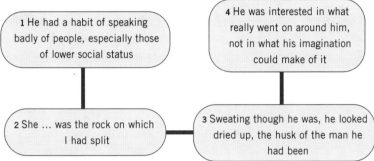

1 He had a habit of speaking badly of people, especially those of lower social status

4 He was interested in what really went on around him, not in what his imagination could make of it

2 She ... was the rock on which I had split

3 Sweating though he was, he looked dried up, the husk of the man he had been

Identify 'to what' this comment refers.

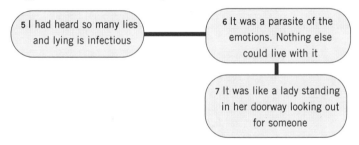

5 I had heard so many lies and lying is infectious

6 It was a parasite of the emotions. Nothing else could live with it

7 It was like a lady standing in her doorway looking out for someone

Check your answers on page 82.

 B *Consider these issues.*

a The ways in which L.P. Hartley lets us know more about the thoughts and feelings of Ted Burgess in this section.

b Your reactions to Marion when she reveals her unhappiness to Leo (Chapter 20).

c The ways in which L.P. Hartley builds up the tension in this section, leading up to the final discovery of Marion and Ted.

d Leo's state of mind and changing emotions, including his motives for resorting to his 'spell'.

e Leo's problems in understanding adult phraseology, and what it tells us about him.

Part five

Epilogue

Leo links his own fate with that of Ted.

The story now returns to a point some months after the adult Leo found his diary. He remembers how he felt during the nervous breakdown which followed the final discovery of Marion and Ted. Despite his mother's reassurances, the young Leo felt responsible for what happened; that he had somehow let everybody down. He was especially upset by the manner of Ted's death. It did not occur to him that perhaps the adults had treated him badly. He felt that in destroying the belladonna plant, he had destroyed Ted, and, in a way, also destroyed his own life. His experiences at Brandham Hall have inhibited him ever since. He has retreated into what he thought of as a safe world of facts and his emotional life has been totally repressed.

Is the past 'another country'? Leo reconsiders.

Looking back, Leo now realises that both Trimingham and Marion did not simply make a fuss of him so that he would run errands, although Marion quickly exploited his potential. He is less sure about Ted's attitude to him, though he was the only one to offer any apology. It must, he realises, have been Marcus who told his mother that Leo had boasted he knew where Marion was when she said she visited her old nanny. Leo is forced to recognise his own share of responsibility for what happened all those years ago and not simply think of himself as a victim of the others. Going over the long-repressed memories of 1900 has finally helped him come to terms with the past. He still has the last letter, which he now reads, only to discover that the present of the bicycle was also intended to assist him in his role of messenger. He decides to try to fill in the missing fifty years between his last memory of Brandham Hall and the present day and returns to Norfolk.

In the church he discovers a memorial to Hugh who died in 1910, and is puzzled by a memorial to a tenth viscount and his wife. He does not realise until later in the day that he was actually Marion's son by Ted, whom Trimingham has accepted as his own. Leo finally finds some kind of peace by praying for all those who were involved in the events of so long ago, including himself.

Wandering through the village, he meets Marion's grandson, and is suddenly struck by the likeness between him and Ted Burgess. Leo is surprised to discover that Marion is still alive and living in Nanny Robson's old house. He hesitates to visit her without prior warning and her grandson reluctantly agrees to explain about Leo's arrival. He senses some kind of tension between Marion and her grandson, who does not see his grandmother very often. He also finds out that Marion has led a very lonely life. On his return, young Ted brings a message from Marion saying that she was not to blame. Replying in Trimingham's words (see Chapter 14), Leo hints that he knows who the young man's grandfather really was. Young Ted suddenly connects the elderly man in front of him with the boy he has heard about. He tries to apologise (like his grandfather before him) but Leo does not want him to feel guilty.

Marion's experiences of the twentieth century have also turned out to be very disappointing.

When he meets Marion, he is shocked by her appearance. In response to his questions she tells him of the deaths of both Marcus and Denys in the First World War, of her mother's permanent nervous breakdown, and of the deaths of her son and daughter-in-law. She pretends to have been very happy and popular, but Leo realises that even he has had a happier life than hers. The past is still causing pain as her grandson refuses to marry a cousin he loves because he feels the family is cursed in some way. She wants Leo

to explain to Ted (or Hugh as he prefers to be called)
how passionate and beautiful her affair with Ted
Burgess was, and that neither she, nor her grandson has
anything to be ashamed of. She pours out all her
feelings to Leo, yearning to see her grandson happily
married, and urging Leo to find love even at this late
stage of his life.

Leo prepares to act At last Leo manages to say goodbye. He is both moved
as a go-between by all that Marion has said, and amazed at the extent
once more. to which she deceives herself about both the past and
the present. He is tempted to excuse himself from
having lunch with young Edward, but goes all the
same. As he drives up to the house, he sees, as he did
when he first arrived in 1900, the 'good side' of the
house, the south-west prospect (see Chapter 2) and we
are left to imagine what Leo will say to Edward over
lunch.

COMMENT   The Epilogue rounds off the story in a number of ways:
- Leo comes to terms with, and re-evaluates the past
  and his role in events
- There is a sense of reconciliation
- It seems likely that Leo's final errand as a go-between
  will be successful and the 'curse' on the family will be
  lifted – a 'happy ending'

- We find out what has happened to all the major characters which gives the reader a sense of completeness. We also see the consequences of the story we have just been told
- We now realise why the Leo pictured in the Prologue has been so disappointed by the twentieth century and why he became the person he is.

GLOSSARY   **Ancient Mariner** a character famous for his long-winded story-telling in a poem by Coleridge
a great deal of manner a slightly exaggerated or affected kind of behaviour

TEST YOURSELF (Part Five: Epilogue)

A *Identify the person 'to whom' this comment refers.*

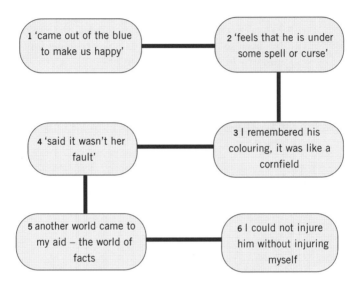

1 'came out of the blue to make us happy'

2 'feels that he is under some spell or curse'

4 'said it wasn't her fault'

3 I remembered his colouring, it was like a cornfield

5 another world came to my aid – the world of facts

6 I could not injure him without injuring myself

Check your answers on page 82.

B *Consider these issues.*

a Whether the epilogue affects your feelings about Marion.

b Whether you think the novel can he described as having a happy ending.

c Whether or not you feel sorry for Leo and the way his life has turned out.

d Some people told L.P. Hartley that the Epilogue spoilt the story or that it wasn't necessary. Think about your reactions to it.

PART THREE

COMMENTARY

THEMES

GROWING UP

Growing up and the difficult transition from child to adult is the most important theme in the novel. Leo is shown as just beginning to tire of childish amusements like sliding down straw stacks and desperately wanting

Leo tries to be grown up.

to sound grown-up as when he tries to pretend he is a 'chilly mortal' at the tea party. He is flattered when Ted tells him he is brave, and later covers up his ignorance of sex. He hates it when the older people treat him as a child, which is partly why he looks up to both Ted and Trimingham. He both likes being the centre of attention, as at the cricket match, but is also frightened of responsibility or of making a fool of himself. His desire to behave responsibly like an adult leads him into going to say goodbye to Ted, with disastrous consequences. Indeed it was his wish to sound grown-up that made him offer to take the first letter.

But he is still a child in many ways; he lives partly in a world of his own imagination, confusing the world of Brandham Hall with the zodiac. He misunderstands a lot of adult language and attitudes and prefers exploring the rubbish heap or the outhouses to the 'endless talking' of the adults. He and Marcus use schoolboy slang, squabble and fight and run everywhere. When

In many ways Leo is still a schoolboy.

he has his new green suit, he becomes Robin Hood. Like a child he likes to feel special and thinks himself rather more important than he really is. After all, Marion and Ted carried on their affair before he arrived on the scene. He has a child's literal mindedness which leads him to misinterpret such things as the story of the fifth viscount, with dire consequences. In the course of the story he begins to understand that things are rarely as simple or black and white as children often imagine them to be. For example, when he learns that Marion is to be engaged, he assumes the letters will cease. He also has to reassess his inherited attitude to war in the light of what Trimingham says. He tends to think the outside world runs according to the same rules as his school life, and even at the very end of his stay he still resorts to superstition and 'magic' in his attempt to sort out the situation, though his first instinct is to get his mother to 'rescue' him by calling him home. He is also just beginning to develop some sexual awareness. He falls in love with Marion, and sees in both Trimingham and Ted some aspects of the adult male he would like to be. He is both fascinated and repelled by the then taboo subject of the facts of life. He begins to understand that 'spooning' isn't something silly or vulgar, but something special and important, even if it does cause heartbreak as well as happiness.

This is an adolescent's view of sex.

SELF-AWARENESS

Linked to the theme of growing up is the theme of self-awareness. Leo is beginning to feel conscious of himself as an individual and is also beginning to be self-conscious. The tea party shows him aware for the first time how he must look to other people and Marcus constantly reminds him of how his clothes or behaviour will affect how people think about him. He feels awkward on the swimming expedition until Marion uses his costume as a towel and he hates it when Marion cannot understand his pronunciation of Hugh. He is initially horrified at the idea of singing at the concert. It is partly his growing sense of himself as a person which makes him feel responsible for the events he finds himself involved in. He is very hurt when he

There are two aspects of self-awareness.

thinks they have all been mocking his naïvety, and that the green bicycle is the final insult. Marcus on the other hand, is already aware of the significance of appearance and the importance of giving the 'right' impression. He points out to Leo that the difference in their social status means that Trimingham can get away with wearing a made-up bow tie but Leo can't. The idea of appearance is linked throughout the story with the importance of clothes. Ted looks best when swimming, nearly naked, but awkward when dressed in his best suit. Trimingham wears his clothes with an easy elegance which reflects his unassuming but assured manner. Leo frequently finds problems with the dress code of the period and his various outfits represent different facets of his character. The constraints on Marion preventing her from doing what she would really like to do are echoed in the restrictive clothes of the period.

Clothes reflects personality and status.

BETRAYAL OF INNOCENCE

This too is a central theme of the novel. L.P. Hartley himself used this phrase to describe the way that Leo was treated by Marion and Ted. Although they had been carrying on their affair before Leo's arrival, they increasingly relied upon him and put pressure on him when he tried to stop. Both used emotional blackmail, though Ted also offered the bribe of the haystack and later the promise to explain about sex. Ted seems to have had some qualms about the strain they were putting on Leo, and did realise that it was Marion who had made Leo cry, though he then went on to try and excuse her. Ted also treated Leo almost as an equal and did honestly try to get him to understand a little about adult emotions. Certainly Leo does not feel so exploited by Ted, whose death grieves him.

Where does the blame lie?

Marion's responsibility on the other hand is perhaps greater. However kind her original motives in befriending Leo, she quickly realised his potential as a messenger. She shows no awareness that he might be finding his role as a messenger a strain once Marcus has recovered or that it might not be morally right to involve a boy as young as Leo. She encourages his obvious devotion to her and she makes him her 'little lamb'. She knows how naïve he is and unused to the ways of adults but she has no qualms about encouraging him to tell lies on her behalf. Unlike Ted, who tries to explain to Leo something of the joy of love, Marion burdens him with her misery and her dilemma in, for example, her outburst over how hard the beds are at Brandham. When he tries to explain why he can no longer act as messenger, she lashes him with her tongue and insults him, only ever offering a half apology for her actions. It is her recklessness, together with her noisy insistence on his taking the final letter which arouses Mrs Maudsley's suspicions about Leo's involvement in the affair, ultimately leading to the trauma of his witnessing the scene in the outhouse.

Note the ambiguity of Marion's attitude to Leo.

Even at the end of the novel, she is unwilling to accept any responsibility for what happened. She does not seem to be aware that is at least partly her fault that Leo has recoiled from the world of the emotions. Nor does she seem able to understand the distress of her grandson. She is self-centred to the end.

MEMORY AND THE IMPORTANCE OF THE PAST

This is an important theme as shown by the words L.P. Hartley uses to open the story. Before we know any details we are aware that the past has had a profound effect on this elderly man. We know some of the outcomes before we learn of the events, and even in the Epilogue, we see Leo still trying to come to terms with the past. This idea is reinforced by his meeting with young Edward, whose life is also being affected by these past events. There is also the added impact of the events of the twentieth century (a past which we as readers can also partly share), which has added to Leo's sense of disillusion and disappointment.

The past must be acknowledged.

Leo's memory for a long time blanked out the past, understandably perhaps, but L.P. Hartley implies, through the life Leo has subsequently led, that this was not a very healthy state of affairs. As he relives the past he is able to get the events into a better perspective, having for too long seen himself either as a guilty party, or as a victim. Marion's grandson too refuses to talk to her about the past, and is miserable as a result. The end of the novel suggests that Leo will be able to help him too to understand the situation.

Marion's life is overshadowed by the past.

There is a kind of **irony** (see Literary Terms) in that Marion used Nanny Robson's poor memory as an excuse for forgetting her visits, when she was actually meeting Ted, and now Marion is living in Nanny Robson's cottage, with her own memories for company, memories which are in many ways as distorted as Leo's; she sees her relationship with Ted in a very rosy, romantic light, forgetting its more sordid aspects.

The more distant past also plays a part in the novel. The fate of the fifth viscount for so many years influences Leo's responses to the situation he finds himself in, and it is partly to save Trimingham from a similar fate that he changes the message and casts the spell.

Structure

ORGANISATION

The novel is rather unusually divided into three parts. This structure has an effect on the way the novel deals with time and the way in which it is linked to the themes of the novel (see Themes).

We see the consequences of events before we find out the causes.

The Prologue starts in the present i.e. the time that the older Leo finds the diary. Through his memories, we find out about his home background, and in particular his experiences at school. These are the formative experiences which explain his attitudes and responses to the events at Brandham Hall. Usually readers are left in suspense about what happens next, but L.P. Hartley wants us to know something of the consequences before we discover any real information about the events which caused them. He lets us know just enough to excite our curiosity but there is still suspense as we don't know any details.

Chapters 1–23 have events taking place in chronological order from the invitation to visit Brandham Hall until the fateful afternoon of Leo's birthday. Even here, there are reminders at various stages of the final **catastrophe** (see Literary Terms).

The story ends where it begins.

The Epilogue takes up the story from the final events of Chapter 23 and tells us what happened in the end. Because his memories end in 1900, the story then carries forward to the present, as Leo returns, as an old man, to Brandham to fill in the missing details and to bring us up to the present. The end of the novel also brings the story round full circle as Leo once again goes up the drive and sees the 'best' side of the house. He is even preparing to act as a go-between once more.

POINT OF VIEW

Note this double perspective.

The whole story is told though the eyes of the central character. This means that we only see events where Leo is present, and know what he knows. As readers, we only have his version of things and have to 'read between the lines' to understand what the thoughts and feelings of the other characters involved may be. For example, we never see Ted and Marion alone. We also have to be alert as readers because in some ways there are two Leos: the young one who finds so much of adult behaviour puzzling and the adult who is able to reflect and who comments on his child-self. It is the adult Leo who offers us interpretations and makes comments which add to the sense of foreboding and suspense (as indicated above).

CHARACTERS

LEO COLSTON

Leo is an only child in a moderately well-off family. He has been educated at home until the death of his bank manager father after which he goes to boarding school. He is an imaginative child who is fascinated by the signs of the zodiac printed in a special diary he is given for 1900, a year which has particular significance for him as it is a new century and he has great hopes for the future. He does not make friends easily, and when he is bullied at school, has no-one to turn to. In any case, he is very conformist and does not question the schoolboy code of behaviour which demands he sort out his own problems. His success at doing this, with his 'curse', together with the subsequent spell, raises his self-esteem. He half-believes he has magical powers, and when he is also treated as someone special at Brandham Hall, this vanity leads, in part, to his downfall.

Literal-minded
Ingratiating
Trusting
Sensitive
Imaginative
Unsophisticated
Susceptible to
flattery

At nearly thirteen, he is on the verge of adolescence. He is just beginning to be conscious of himself as a person and concerned about how he is seen by others. Without a father, he is searching for someone to act as a role-model. For example, he is both attracted to Ted Burgess's physique and a little afraid it. He also admires Trimingham, though there is some snobbery mixed in as Trimingham is a Lord (whereas Ted is a farmer). He is ignorant of the facts of life but, despite sharing the schoolboy scorn for romantic love he is beginning to be curious about adult relationships. He identifies Marion with the sign of Virgo in his diary, and becomes devoted to her. He is sensitive, both in his own character, and to the feelings of others. He shares the anguish of Marion and Ted, as well as being anxious for the safety of Trimingham. He sympathises with Marion's predicament and it is only through his eyes that we glimpse something of the intensity of feeling between Marion and Ted.

He allows himself to be flattered by the attention Marion gives him and his self-importance grows as he runs his errands, seeing himself as the messenger of the gods. He is very trusting and naïve, and it does not occur to him until it is too late that the adults were in part exploiting him, although he was also eager to sustain his feelings of self-importance. He is a child in an adult world which he does not understand as, for example, in his reactions to the story of the fate of the fifth viscount. His lack of sophistication even extends to their language as he is at times mystified by expressions they take for granted.

He is also quite a serious, thoughtful boy who has been brought up to have a sense of responsibility to others which causes him to suffer guilt for what happens. He is emotionally scarred for life by the events at Brandham Hall although he shows himself even as an adult to be a willing go-between. As an adult, having been deeply hurt in the world of emotions and imagination, he has taken refuge in a life devoted to facts, though he still feels dissatisfied, and even embittered, by the past.

MARION MAUDSLEY

Decisive

Selfish

Thoughtless

Reckless

Basically good-natured

A realist but also self-deluding

Marion is a beautiful young woman from an upper-middle-class family in late-Victorian England, and therefore expected to make a 'good' marriage. There are no other choices open to her. She is not free to follow her own feelings, as she tries to explain to Leo. She is torn between her love for Ted Burgess, and her need to marry Trimingham who will give her the social status she, and her family, want. She is determined and strongwilled (like her mother), but not strong enough, or impractical enough, to publicly defy convention. She genuinely loves Ted, and is prepared to tackle Trimingham when she thinks he is trying to get rid of Ted by getting him to volunteer for the army. She does not want to see Ted hurt, but rather selfishly does not seems to realise that she is hurting him by recklessly continuing the affair, taking increasing risks, which finally results in Ted's death. She is critical of his suicide, having no patience with what she thinks of as weakness.

She has a cruel, heartless streak in her character. She snubs Trimingham on more than one occasion and applauds loudly when he gets out in the cricket match. She turns quite viciously on Leo when he tries to stop taking the messages but her anger is short-lived and she does not seem to realise how much she has hurt him. She does have a good side too. She is basically kind and is the first to realise Leo's problems over his summer clothes, which she handles with tact and sympathy. But the visit to Norwich, like the later birthday bicycle, also shows how resourceful and manipulative she is. She meets Ted in Norwich, and the bicycle is to help Leo take messages. She seems fond of Leo and offers him a sort of apology for her shouting at him, but is also prepared to exploit him rather thoughtlessly, not realising the strain she is putting him under. As an old lady, she is still not prepared to acknowledge any responsibly for what happened to Leo; it is her grandson who apologises. Our feelings about her are perhaps affected by the fact that she is shown to have suffered as a result of her actions; the family history in the twentieth century had not been a happy one, and her grandson is still suffering the consequences of her actions. The self-deception she showed in thinking she could marry Trimingham, and still carry on an affair with Ted continues into old age –she continues to delude herself by thinking she has lots of visitors and is popular.

TED BURGESS

As a working farmer and a tenant, Ted is lower in social status than Marion and this is the stumbling block of their relationship. Through his attempts at explanation of love and 'spooning' we can see the depth of emotion he feels for Marion. He allows himself to be dominated by her, saying it is up to her whether or not he joins the army. Marion calls his behaviour in shooting himself weak, but it call also be seen as an act of bravery in clearing himself out of her way, or showing that his sensitive nature could not live with the gossip. He seems to be a man caught up in a situation which can only lead to disaster, and L.P. Hartley hints at this tragic outcome throughout the telling of the story.

His behaviour at the concert shows he is embarrassed at being the centre of attraction, and it seems that he finds

Inarticulate
Good-natured
Honourable
Sympathetic
Weak-willed
Physically brave
Aware of social
inferiority but not
subservient

carrying on a secret affair very stressful, despite his reputation as a 'lady killer'. At the beginning of the novel his physical strength and vigour are impressive (Leo identifies him with the water-carrier in the zodiac) but Leo observes how he loses weight and seems increasingly drawn as time goes by. He contrasts with Marion in that he has more qualms of conscience about using Leo as a 'postman' although it is he who first employs him as such. He tries to offer Leo something in return, and is shrewd enough to realise that it is Marion who has made Leo cry. He also writes him a genuine letter of apology after he has ordered him out of the house. He does not patronise Leo, but he cannot always find the words to express the complex and difficult ideas Leo wants him to explain. He has his dignity, and gives way at the swimming pond only after he has had one more plunge. It is a tribute to his genuine personality that he is the character that Leo feels most for at the end of the affair.

HUGH, NINTH VISCOUNT TRIMINGHAM

Trimingham is a member of the aristocracy but he does not in any way put on airs and graces. Unlike Marcus, who is very concerned with etiquette, Trimingham tactfully saves Leo from embarrassment over his title and how to address him, and later over the made-up bow tie he has as a birthday present. He is genuinely kind to Leo, patiently answering his questions and not patronising him. He is sensitive to the feelings of a boy who is about to become a teenager. He too employs Leo as a messenger, but not in a way that causes him any emotional stress. In fact he contributes to Leo's feeling special by calling him Mercury. He seems to be genuinely in love with Marion, even though she shows little fondness for him in the novel and at times he seems a bit hurt by her behaviour. He does not seem to

Courteous
Tactful
A war hero
Unassuming
Honourable
Kind

have any mercenary motive in wanting to marry her and later in the Epilogue Marion praises his loyalty to her. His slightly old-fashioned chivalric nature is summed up in the phrase, 'Nothing is ever a lady's fault' though this does have an unfortunate effect on Leo. His quiet, dignified strength of character is shown in the way he brings up Marion's son by Ted as his own. He impresses Leo not just because he is a lord, but also because he is an admirable character. He behaves with impeccable courtesy and tact as a guest in what is his own home, always deferring to his hosts. There is no suggestion that he wants to get Ted out of the way, or even that he suspects anything. He encourages Ted to enlist simply out of patriotism. He has already demonstrated his own bravery as his terribly war-scarred face shows. His early death implies there was other, unrecognised damage. Leo identifies him with the archer in the zodiac. He seems to be a good landlord, treating his tenants with respect and courtesy; Denys dare not order Ted away from the swimming pond because he is Trimingham's tenant.

MARCUS MAUDSLEY

Marcus is a fellow school pupil rather than a close friend of Leo. The measles outbreak, together with his admiration for Leo's 'magic', has brought them together. He is a year younger, but far more sophisticated. A favourite word of criticism is 'boring'. Unlike Leo, he is fascinated by the adult world (including 'spooning') and is a great gossip. It is he who probably tells his mother (to whom he is very close) enough to allow her to guess where Ted and Marion meet. He is a snob who criticises Leo's knowledge of etiquette, dress code, etc. and is disdainful of the lower classes, such as the villagers during the cricket concert. He is more quick-witted than Leo and enjoys

Precocious
Snobbish
Over-bearing
Spiteful
Self-assured
Tells tales

demonstrating his superiority in French. He can be spiteful as when he taunts Leo for being 'green.'

His role in the novel is in part to act as an informant to Leo (and the reader), concerning such events as the forthcoming engagement, and as a contrast to Leo. His self-assurance also highlights Leo's sense of inferiority and insecurity. His illness in part leads to Leo becoming a go-between. He is tragically killed in the First World War.

MRS MAUDSLEY

Initially, Marcus's mother is presented as a very strong character. She has a very piercing eyes which seem to reflect her strong will. Increasingly, the strain of successfully bringing about Marion's engagement to Trimingham begins to show and the final **catastrophe** (see Literary Terms) causes her permanent breakdown. People are not at ease in her company, especially Leo, though she is an attentive and efficient hostess. When she is ill, the house takes on a more relaxed atmosphere. She is not very sensitive to the feelings of others. For example, she makes Leo cry over not having any summer clothes. Marcus is her favourite. She is rather sarcastic to her older son, and there seems to be constant tension between her and Marion. She is partly to blame for Leo's breakdown as she thoughtlessly and ruthlessly drags him with her to the outhouses.

MR MAUDSLEY

Mr Maudsley is a silent, reserved man who has made a lot of money in banking and whose fortune supports his family in some style. He seems at first to be dominated by his wife. It is he who takes the temperature readings which begin to fascinate Leo. The cricket match shows the hidden strength and resourcefulness of his character when he bats unspectacularly, but efficiently, and saves the innings, giving us a hint of the way he will take command of events at the end of the novel. He has some shrewd suspicions of Ted Burgess which Leo overhears but he does not guess the full story until it is too late. He represents the new upper-middle class who have made their own money and are rising in importance compared to the inherited status of the aristocracy.

DENYS MAUDSLEY

Marcus's older brother, is well-meaning but not very intelligent, though he likes to give his very decided opinions when he can. No mention is made of his having any kind of employment. His character is displayed in his enthusiastic but bungling innings at the cricket match. He is in awe of his mother who is very critical of him. He has little to say to Leo, to whom he represents all the young adults in the house whose behaviour Leo does not understand, but Denys's basic good nature is shown when he contributes to Leo's new clothes. A typical member of the snobbish upper-middle class, he is condescending to Ted, because he is Trimingham's tenant. His lack of intelligence and good sense provide a contrast to Trimingham. He is tragically killed in the First World War.

MRS COLSTON

Leo's mother is a gentle, rather shy lady who is has been left a widow with a modest income and who is finding it hard to bring up her son alone. Her reluctance, with Leo's agreement, to spend money on summer clothes meant that he could not cope with the heat wave. They are close but Leo still finds it difficult to confide in her. The **catastrophe** (see Literary Terms) might have been averted if she had responded differently to Leo's two contradictory letters home. She has a very strong sense of what is right and wrong, which she has in some ways passed on to her son.

LANGUAGE & STYLE

Look back at the text and note where the key conversations are.

The main style of language is that of the adult narrator, though L.P. Hartley does let us hear the voices of all the central characters by using quite a lot of dialogue. The letters included in the narrative also tell us more about some of the characters, e.g. Mrs Colston and Ted; they also show how much of a child Leo still is. His conversations with Marcus especially, with their schoolboy French, insults and slang, remind us that they are both young boys.

A very important aspect of style in *The Go-Between* is the use of **symbols** (see Literary Terms) and you have been asked to think about some of these as you have worked through these notes. L.P. Hartley thought that the three most important symbols were the deadly nightshade, the landscape and the climate. The following are only brief notes to give you the basis on which to make more detailed notes of your own.

The deadly nightshade: the deadly nightshade symbolises the relationship between Marion and Ted, beautiful but dangerous, even deadly. It grows as their passion increases. Leo is both fascinated and afraid of it; aware that it is dangerous though he doesn't want to tell Mrs Maudsley about it. In the end, Leo believes he has to destroy the plant to put an end to the affair.

The landscape: the social gulf between Marion and Ted is reflected in the distance between the house and the farm, with the river as a kind of crossing point. Leo first sees Ted here at the sluice-gate where he is an 'outsider' intruding on the world of the Hall. Leo's role as a 'go -between' involves his journeying back and forth through woodland, which is often the place where he has his bleaker thoughts and open country where he once again comes under the influence of the heat. The harvest and the corn field symbolise Ted's fate. The landscape becomes increasingly arid and dried up as the story unfolds and Leo himself seems to subconsciously link this with the destructive nature of the situation he finds himself in. Brandham Hall itself can also be seen as a symbol. For example, Leo cannot remember its 'best' side until the very end of the novel. There are two separate 'worlds': the showy front of the house where the entertaining takes place and the back of the house with its passages and outhouses, where the servants (and Leo) feel more at home. Even the impressive double staircase shows Leo's childish superstition. Ted's farmhouse is in direct contrast and shows his different social status. Even Leo's changes of bedroom reflect his differing circumstances and emotional experiences.

The climate: the climate is linked with the emotions of the central characters which it both seems to affect and reflect. At first the heat is Leo's 'enemy', echoing his sense of insecurity, but then it becomes the new environment for his new personality. When matters reach a head, Leo sees the cooler weather as a sign that things are returning to normal. The actual crisis occurs against the ominous background of the thunderstorm and the impending disaster is hinted at by the cloud which hangs over the cricket field. The heat is also seen as increasingly destructive, as shown in the various stages of the drying up of the river. The hot weather is seen as 'unnatural' reflecting the extraordinary events of the story.

Part four

Study skills

How to use quotations

One of the secrets of success in writing essays is the way you use quotations. There are five basic principles:

- Put inverted commas at the beginning and end of the quotation
- Write the quotation exactly as it appears in the original
- Do not use a quotation that repeats what you have just written
- Use the quotation so that it fits into your sentence
- Keep the quotation as short as possible

Quotations should be used to develop the line of thought in your essays.

Your comment should not duplicate what is in your quotation. For example:

> Leo tells us how he was sweating when he says, 'my face flamed while it dripped'.

Far more effective is to write:

> Leo shows us how hot with embarrassment he was when he says, 'My face flamed while it dripped'.

The most sophisticated way of using the writer's words is to embed them into your sentence:

> The fact that he now thinks of himself as 'a figure of fun' and feels 'utterly out of place among these smart rich people' shows us just how much of an outsider Leo now feels himself to be.

When you use quotations in this way, you are demonstrating the ability to use text as evidence to support your ideas - not simply including words from the original to prove you have read it.

Everyone writes differently. Work through the suggestions given here and adapt the advice to suit your own style and interests. This will improve your essay-writing skills and allow your personal voice to emerge.

The following points indicate in ascending order the skills of essay writing:

- Picking out one or two facts about the story and adding the odd detail
- Writing about the text by retelling the story
- Retelling the story and adding a quotation here and there
- Organising an answer which explains what is happening in the text and giving quotations to support what you write

....

- Writing in such a way as to show that you have thought about the intentions of the writer of the text and that you understand the techniques used
- Writing at some length, giving your viewpoint on the text and commenting by picking out details to support your views
- Looking at the text as a work of art, demonstrating clear critical judgement and explaining to the reader of your essay how the enjoyment of the text is assisted by literary devices, linguistic effects and psychological insights; showing how the text relates to the time when it was written

The dotted line above represents the division between lower and higher level grades. Higher-level performance begins when you start to consider your response as a reader of the text. The highest level is reached when you offer an enthusiastic personal response and show how this piece of literature is a product of its time.

Coursework essay

Set aside an hour or so at the start of your work to plan what you have to do.

- List all the points you feel are needed to cover the task. Collect page references of information and quotations that will support what you have to say. A helpful tool is the highlighter pen: this saves painstaking copying and enables you to target precisely what you want to use.
- Focus on what you consider to be the main points of the essay. Try to sum up your argument in a single sentence, which could be the closing sentence of your essay. Depending on the essay title, it could be a statement about a character: Leo claims that after the events of the summer of 1900 he vowed 'never to meddle for good or ill in other people's business' but his actions at the end of the novel show that he cannot resist the invitation to be a go-between once again; an opinion about setting: I think that Leo is still a young boy is summed up by the fact that he prefers the back stairs and the dilapidated outhouses which he can explore at will, to the grand rooms and formal gardens which the adults enjoy; or a judgement on a theme: Hartley uses Leo's changing attitude to sliding down the haystack as one way of exploring the theme of his growing up and tiring of childish activities.
- Make a short essay plan. Use the first paragraph to introduce the argument you wish to make. In the following paragraphs develop this argument with details, examples and other possible points of view. Sum up your argument in the last paragraph. Check you have answered the question.
- Write the essay, remembering all the time the central point you are making.
- On completion, go back over what you have written to eliminate careless errors and improve expression. Read it aloud to yourself, or, if you are feeling more confident, to a relative or friend.

If you can, try to type your essay, using a word processor. This will allow you to correct and improve your writing without spoiling its appearance.

Examination
essay

The essay written in an examination often carries more marks than the coursework essay even though it is written under considerable time pressure.

In the revision period build up notes on various aspects of the text you are using. Fortunately, in acquiring this set of York Notes on *The Go-Between*, you have made a prudent beginning! York Notes are set out to give you vital information and help you to construct your personal overview of the text.

Make notes with appropriate quotations about the key issues of the set text. Go into the examination knowing your text and having a clear set of opinions about it.

In most English Literature examinations, you can take in copies of your set books. This is an enormous advantage although it may lull you into a false sense of security. Beware! There is simply not enough time in an examination to read the book from scratch.

In the
examination

- Read the question paper carefully and remind yourself what you have to do.
- Look at the questions on your set texts to select the one that most interests you and mentally work out the points you wish to stress.
- Remind yourself of the time available and how you are going to use it.
- Briefly map out a short plan in note form that will keep your writing on track and illustrate the key argument you want to make.
- Then set about writing it.
- When you have finished, check through to eliminate errors.

To summarise,
these are the
keys to success:

- **Know the text**
- **Have a clear understanding of and opinions on the storyline, characters, setting, themes and writer's concerns**
- **Select the right material**
- **Plan and write a clear response, continually bearing the question in mind**

SAMPLE ESSAY PLAN

A typical essay question on *The Go-Between* is followed by a sample essay plan in note form. This does not present the only answer to the question, so do not be afraid to include your own ideas, or exclude some of the following. Remember that quotations are essential to prove and illustrate the points you make.

What are the key stages in Leo's development towards adulthood?

- At school he learns that he must sort out his own problems and cannot rely on others to help him. He must also face up to the consequences of his own, rash actions.
- At the tea party he becomes, for the first time, conscious of how he looks. He also gradually understands the significance of clothes as badges of social status. He begins to understand about etiquette and the rules which govern polite society. His subsequent conversations with both Ted and especially Trimingham develop these ideas. The story of the fifth viscount introduces him to a code of honour and responsibility for the actions of others.
- The bathing party shows his awakening awareness of adult bodies and he begins to fall in love with Marion. His understanding of love and sex is later explored in his conversations with Ted and Marcus about 'spooning', and his reading of the unsealed letter.

- At the cricket match Leo has to change from being a spectator to taking an active role. He has to shoulder the responsibility of making the catch. He also realises many of the undercurrents in the behaviour of the adults on this occasion. The experience is in some ways duplicated in the concert where he is again faced with what seems to be a daunting task which he handles successfully.
- Marcus's comments about the green bicycle as well as his earlier present of the clothes force him to face up to his own weaknesses and immaturity. He has to try and reassess his feelings about Marion, especially after she reveals to him something of her unhappiness and suffering. He also has to think through his feelings about Ted and Trimingham at various stages in the story.
- At the end of the visit, he has gone too far in assuming an adult sense of responsibility for events as he tries to control them. He suffers a nervous breakdown in growing up too quickly. Later, we learn that he has never developed any close emotional ties, and has taken refuge in a life spent dealing only in facts. His final 'growing up' could be said to take place when he faces up to the past, and revisits Norfolk.

FURTHER QUESTIONS

Here are more questions on the novel. Work out what your answer would be, always being sure to draw up a plan first.

1 'Nothing is ever a lady's fault'. Do you think this is true of Marion?

2 Consider the special significance of the cricket match and the supper which follows. How do these events link to the key themes in the novel?

3 Describe some of the ways in which Leo misunderstands language or expressions used by the adults and discuss their significance for both character and plot.

4 Marion describes Ted as 'weak'. What is your assessment of his character?

5 Compare the tea-time episode in Chapter 3 with tea-time in Chapter 4, and discuss Leo's 'transformation' of character and outlook.

6 How much do you think Leo was to blame for what happened? Is he a natural go-between?

7 Compare and contrast Leo's attitude to and feelings towards Ted and Trimingham. Make sure you support your comments with examples or references to the story.

8 Describe the significance of the weather in the novel.

9 What do you think the novel gains (or loses) by having a Prologue and an Epilogue?

10 Why do you think Leo has become so infatuated with Marion? Give reasons for your comments.

11 Discuss the significance of the various letters in the novel.

12 In what ways are Leo's experiences at school important for later events in the novel?

13 Describe the relationship between Leo and Marcus. Could they ever have become real friends?

14 What do you think L.P. Hartley's use of **symbols** (see Literary Terms) adds to the novel?

PART FIVE

CULTURAL CONNECTIONS

BROADER PERSPECTIVES

Film   Try to see Joseph Losey's film of *The Go-Between* with a screenplay by Harold Pinter (1971). A useful exercise would be to note the differences between the film and the novel, and think about their effect. It is also full of accurate period details which will help you visualise the landscape and the house.

Another film adaption of a novel which deals with the experiences of an outsider in a great country house (though a little later in date) is *The Remains of the Day* (1993). This also will give you some insight into the way of life and the importance of class, etc

Written works   *Great Expectations* by Charles Dickens (Penguin Classics, 1996 – first published 1861) is another novel dealing with childhood experiences told from the point of view of an adult looking back.

Mention has already been made to L.P. Hartley's admiration for Emily Brönte's *Wuthering Heights* (Penguin Classics, 1996 – first published 1847) (see L.P. Hartley's Background) which also deals with the past in the context of the present.

Another novel which tells us almost the end of the story first and then goes back to various periods in the past is Paul Scott's *Staying On* (1977) (which is also available in a television adaptation).

For more information and illustrations of the setting of the story, you could consult *Life in the English Country House*, by Mark Girourard (1978).

If you have the opportunity, try to visit one of the large country houses open to the public, where you can experience what life was like at the turn of the century.

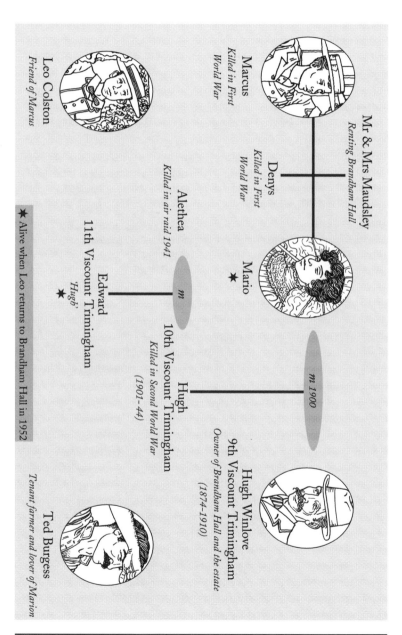

Mr & Mrs Maudsley
Renting Brandham Hall

Marcus
Killed in First World War

Denys
Killed in First World War

Alethea
Killed in air raid 1941

★ **Mario**

Edward
11th Viscount Trimingham
'Hugh' ★

m

Hugh
10th Viscount Trimingham
Killed in Second World War (1901–44)

m 1900

Hugh Winlove
9th Viscount Trimingham
Owner of Brandham Hall and the estate (1874–1910)

Leo Colston
Friend of Marcus

Ted Burgess
Tenant farmer and lover of Marion

★ Alive when Leo returns to Brandham Hall in 1952

catastrophe the crisis point which a series of related events has been building up to, such as the discovery of Marion and Ted in the outhouse

denouement the final outcome of a complex set of circumstances such as the events detailed in the Epilogue

irony the use of words which express the opposite of the meaning intended; when used as an adjective (ironic) it suggests a situation which has turned out the opposite of what might have been expected. For example, Leo feels that it is ironic that a Norfolk jacket should be out of place in Norfolk

metaphor a description of something in terms of something else; a comparison without the use of 'like'. For example, Mrs Maudsley's piercing dark eyes are compared to a 'black searchlight', suggesting the intensity of her gaze which Leo cannot escape from

pun a humorous play on words, which exploits the fact that words may sound the same but have different meanings, as when Denys says 'Bags I the bags' where bags refers to both trousers and choosing something

symbol an object or a situation to represent an idea or set of ideas. For example, the belladonna plant symbolises Marion and the sexual relationship which she has with Ted, at once both beautiful and vigorous but also potentially poisonous and destructive. Leo feels impelled to destroy it to break up the relationship

TEST ANSWERS

TEST YOURSELF (Part One)

A...
1 Jenkins and Strode *(Prologue)*
2 Marion and her mother *(Chapter 3)*
3 Ted Burgess *(Chapter 4)*
4 Trimingham *(Chapter 6)*
5 At school *(Prologue)*
6 At the tea party *(Chapter 3)*
7 After Leo gets his new clothes *(Chapter 4)*
8 Leo lends Marion his bathing costume *(Chapter 4)*

TEST YOURSELF (Part Two)

A...
1 Ted *(Chapter 10)*
2 Trimingham *(Chapter 8)*
3 Leo *(Chapter 8)*
4 Leo after reading the letter *(Chapter 10)*
5 Ted, reading in the cornfield *(Chapter 9)*
6 Leo to Ted, after bandaging Leo's knee *(Chapter 7)*
7 Marion to Leo after receiving the first letter *(Chapter 7)*

TEST YOURSELF (Part Three)

A...
1 Leo at the cricket match *(Chapter 12)*

2 Marion when Leo refuses to take a letter *(Chapter 15)*
3 Marion and Ted at the concert *(Chapter 13)*
4 Leo writes home asking to be recalled *(Chapter 17)*
5 Leo about Ted, after the concert and the cricket match *(Chapter 14)*
6 Leo changes Trimingham's message *(Chapter 11)*

TEST YOURSELF (Part Four)

A...
1 Marcus *(Chapter 19)*
2 Marion *(Chapter 20)*
3 Ted *(Chapter 19)*
4 Marcus *(Chapter 22)*
5 Leo's lie about the swimming lesson *(Chapter 19)*
6 The relationship between Ted and Marion *(Chapter 21)*
7 The belladonna plant *(Chapter 21)*

TEST YOURSELF (Part Five)

A...
1 Leo
2 Young Edward
3 Young Edward
4 Marion
5 Leo
6 Ted Burgess

NOTES

NOTES

Notes

NOTES

Notes

NOTES

NOTES

Notes

GCSE and equivalent levels (£3.50 each)

Maya Angelou
I Know Why the Caged Bird Sings

Jane Austen
Pride and Prejudice

Harold Brighouse
Hobson's Choice

Charlotte Brontë
Jane Eyre

Emily Brontë
Wuthering Heights

Charles Dickens
David Copperfield

Charles Dickens
Great Expectations

Charles Dickens
Hard Times

George Eliot
Silas Marner

William Golding
Lord of the Flies

Willis Hall
The Long and the Short and the Tall

Thomas Hardy
Far from the Madding Crowd

Thomas Hardy
The Mayor of Casterbridge

Thomas Hardy
Tess of the d'Urbervilles

L.P. Hartley
The Go-Between

Seamus Heaney
Selected Poems

Susan Hill
I'm the King of the Castle

Barry Hines
A Kestrel for a Knave

Louise Lawrence
Children of the Dust

Harper Lee
To Kill a Mockingbird

Laurie Lee
Cider with Rosie

Arthur Miller
A View from the Bridge

Arthur Miller
The Crucible

Robert O'Brien
Z for Zachariah

George Orwell
Animal Farm

J.B. Priestley
An Inspector Calls

Willy Russell
Educating Rita

Willy Russell
Our Day Out

J.D. Salinger
The Catcher in the Rye

William Shakespeare
Henry V

William Shakespeare
Julius Caesar

William Shakespeare
Macbeth

William Shakespeare
A Midsummer Night's Dream

William Shakespeare
The Merchant of Venice

William Shakespeare
Romeo and Juliet

William Shakespeare
The Tempest

William Shakespeare
Twelfth Night

George Bernard Shaw
Pygmalion

R.C. Sherriff
Journey's End

Rukshana Smith
Salt on the snow

John Steinbeck
Of Mice and Men

R.L. Stevenson
Dr Jekyll and Mr Hyde

Robert Swindells
Daz 4 Zoe

Mildred D. Taylor
Roll of Thunder, Hear My Cry

Mark Twain
The Adventures of Huckleberry Finn

James Watson
Talking in Whispers

A Choice of Poets

Nineteenth Century Short Stories

Poetry of the First World War

Six Women Poets

Advanced level (£3.99 each)

Margaret Atwood
The Handmaid's Tale

William Blake
Songs of Innocence and of Experience

Emily Brontë
Wuthering Heights

Geoffrey Chaucer
The Wife of Bath's Prologue and Tale

Joseph Conrad
Heart of Darkness

Charles Dickens
Great Expectations

F. Scott Fitzgerald
The Great Gatsby

Thomas Hardy
Tess of the d'Urbervilles

James Joyce
Dubliners

Arthur Miller
Death of a Salesman

William Shakespeare
Antony and Cleopatra

William Shakespeare
Hamlet

William Shakespeare
King Lear

William Shakespeare
The Merchant of Venice

William Shakespeare
Romeo and Juliet

William Shakespeare
The Tempest

Mary Shelley
Frankenstein

Alice Walker
The Color Purple

Tennessee Williams
A Streetcar Named Desire

Jane Austen
Emma

William Shakespeare
Much Ado About Nothing

Jane Austen
Pride and Prejudice

William Shakespeare
Othello

Charlotte Brontë
Jane Eyre

John Webster
The Duchess of Malfi

Seamus Heaney
Selected Poems

Chinua Achebe
Things Fall Apart

Edward Albee
Who's Afraid of Virginia Woolf?

Jane Austen
Mansfield Park

Jane Austen
Northanger Abbey

Jane Austen
Persuasion

Jane Austen
Sense and Sensibility

Samuel Beckett
Waiting for Godot

Alan Bennett
Talking Heads

John Betjeman
Selected Poems

Robert Bolt
A Man for All Seasons

Robert Burns
Selected Poems

Lord Byron
Selected Poems

Geoffrey Chaucer
The Franklin's Tale

Geoffrey Chaucer
The Merchant's Tale

Geoffrey Chaucer
The Miller's Tale

Geoffrey Chaucer
The Nun's Priest's Tale

Geoffrey Chaucer
Prologue to the Canterbury Tales

Samuel Taylor Coleridge
Selected Poems

Daniel Defoe
Moll Flanders

Daniel Defoe
Robinson Crusoe

Shelagh Delaney
A Taste of Honey

Charles Dickens
Bleak House

Charles Dickens
Oliver Twist

Emily Dickinson
Selected Poems

John Donne
Selected Poems

Douglas Dunn
Selected Poems

George Eliot
Middlemarch

George Eliot
The Mill on the Floss

T.S. Eliot
The Waste Land

T.S. Eliot
Selected Poems

Henry Fielding
Joseph Andrews

E.M. Forster
Howards End

E.M. Forster
A Passage to India

John Fowles
The French Lieutenant's Woman

Brian Friel
Translations

Elizabeth Gaskell
North and South

Oliver Goldsmith
She Stoops to Conquer

Graham Greene
Brighton Rock

Thomas Hardy
Jude the Obscure

Thomas Hardy
Selected Poems

Nathaniel Hawthorne
The Scarlet Letter

Ernest Hemingway
The Old Man and the Sea

Homer
The Iliad

Homer
The Odyssey

Aldous Huxley
Brave New World

Ben Jonson
The Alchemist

Ben Jonson
Volpone

James Joyce
A Portrait of the Artist as a Young Man

John Keats
Selected Poems

Philip Larkin
Selected Poems

D.H. Lawrence
The Rainbow

D.H. Lawrence
Sons and Lovers

D.H. Lawrence
Women in Love

Christopher Marlowe
Doctor Faustus

John Milton
Paradise Lost Bks I & II

John Milton
Paradise Lost IV & IX

Sean O'Casey
Juno and the Paycock

George Orwell
Nineteen Eighty-four

John Osborne
Look Back in Anger

Wilfred Owen
Selected Poems

Harold Pinter
The Caretaker

Sylvia Plath
Selected Works

Alexander Pope
Selected Poems

Jean Rhys
Wide Sargasso Sea

William Shakespeare
As You Like It

William Shakespeare
Coriolanus

William Shakespeare
Henry IV Pt 1

William Shakespeare
Henry V

William Shakespeare
Julius Caesar

William Shakespeare
Measure for Measure

William Shakespeare
Much Ado About Nothing

William Shakespeare
A Midsummer Night's Dream

William Shakespeare
Richard II

William Shakespeare
Richard III

William Shakespeare
Sonnets

William Shakespeare
The Taming of the Shrew

William Shakespeare
The Winter's Tale

George Bernard Shaw
Arms and the Man

George Bernard Shaw
Saint Joan

Richard Brinsley Sheridan
The Rivals

Muriel Spark
The Prime of Miss Jean Brodie

John Steinbeck
The Grapes of Wrath

John Steinbeck
The Pearl

Tom Stoppard
*Rosencrantz and Guildenstern
are Dead*

Jonathan Swift
Gulliver's Travels

John Millington Synge
*The Playboy of the Western
World*

W.M. Thackeray
Vanity Fair

Virgil
The Aeneid

Derek Walcott
Selected Poems

Oscar Wilde
*The Importance of Being
Earnest*

Tennessee Williams
Cat on a Hot Tin Roof

Tennessee Williams
The Glass Menagerie

Virginia Woolf
Mrs Dalloway

Virginia Woolf
To the Lighthouse

William Wordsworth
Selected Poems

W.B. Yeats
Selected Poems

York Notes – the Ultimate Literature Guides

York Notes are recognised as the best literature study guides.
If you have enjoyed using this book and have found it useful, you
can now order others directly from us – simply follow the ordering
instructions below.

HOW TO ORDER

Decide which title(s) you require and then order in one of the following
ways:

Booksellers
All titles available from good bookstores.

By post
List the title(s) you require in the space provided overleaf,
select your method of payment, complete your name and
address details and return your completed order form and
payment to:

> *Addison Wesley Longman Ltd*
> *PO BOX 88*
> *Harlow*
> *Essex CM19 5SR*

By phone
Call our Customer Information Centre on 01279 623923 to
place your order, quoting mail number: HEYN1.

By fax
Complete the order form overleaf, ensuring you fill in your
name and address details and method of payment, and fax it
to us on 01279 414130.

By e-mail
E-mail your order to us on awlhe.orders@awl.co.uk listing
title(s) and quantity required and providing full name and
address details as requested overleaf. Please quote mail
number: HEYN1. Please do not send credit card details by
e-mail.

York Notes Order Form

Titles required:

Quantity	Title/ISBN	Price

Sub total _____

Please add £2.50 postage & packing _____

(*P & P is free for orders over £50*) _____

Total _____

Mail no: HEYN1

Your Name _____

Your Address _____

_____

Postcode _____   Telephone _____

Method of payment

☐ I enclose a cheque or a P/O for £_____ made payable to Addison Wesley Longman Ltd

☐ Please charge my Visa/Access/AMEX/Diners Club card
Number _____   Expiry Date _____
Signature _____   Date _____

(please ensure that the address given above is the same as for your credit card)

Prices and other details are correct at time of going to press but may change without notice. All orders are subject to status.

☐ *Please tick this box if you would like a complete listing of Longman Study Guides (suitable for GCSE and A-level students)*

 York Press

Longman

Addison Wesley Longman